I0660305

COVER ME

The Loyalty Treasures

Mark Arnold

Cover Me Movement Edition

Now a full-length feature film!

TABLE OF CONTENTS

DEDICATION

At the time of the release of this Cover Me Movement Edition publication, the world in general and the United States in particular faces struggles internally. This manual is dedicated to all those who openly and willingly embrace the desire and effort to change the world, by changing their community by changing – themselves.

If we are willing to turn to God every day and ask how we can better love our neighbors, we have a chance. And as my friend and associate Kenneth Brandy says, "I woke up with a chance."

To God be the glory!

SPONSORS

For more details go to :

https://cutt.ly/MiracleCoverMeSelection

https://cutt.ly/HappyCoffee

PROLOGUE

Michael walked up to the door to their room. He knocked lightly. From within he could hear Marie invitingly say, "Come in." He entered the room, closing the door behind him. Michael's eyes adjusted to the multi-candle lit room. Marie had turned off the lights and had placed several candles around the room for a more romantic setting.

"What is that you have with you there, Michael Stoneman? Bribery of some sort, I assume?" Marie smiled. She was wearing a set of footie pajamas that he had bought for her, not quite buttoned all the way. Michael was not one of those fantasy outfit kind of guys. From high school he had loved Marie for who she was in her caring ways.

"If bribery is what it takes to steal your heart away, my love, then bribery it is!" Michael set the tray at the end of the bed on the bench that was there for putting on one's shoes. They each seated themselves on the end of the bed. POP!!! It was the sound of the cork as Michael opened the champagne and poured them each a glass. As they raised their glasses, Michael said, "To the most wonderful and lovely wife any man could ever have, and who I love now and will love with all my heart forever." They tapped their glasses in a toast, and each took a healthy sip.

"I think this is working Michael," Marie said with a smile as she leaned forward to kiss Michael with a deep breathed kiss. "Here we are on this lovely 'cruise' on the 'USS Loyalty' - I could get used to this." The room swayed slightly as their "vessel" moved in the night, and the warm breezes pressed against the windows.

"Marie, I hope that is true. I don't want to belabor the point, but I want to say I am sorry." Michael reached out and took her one hand.

"Sorry for what, honey? You planning to eat all of those strawberries by yourself?" Marie was poking some fun at Michael, trying to let him know she understood. Michael smiled, picked up one of the strawberries, and brushed it gently on her lips just enough so she could taste the chocolate. As she tried to take a bite, he pulled it away slightly. After a few of these playful retreats, he let her enjoy the wonderful flavor of the dark chocolate over the fresh strawberry. "Mmmm," was all she could manage with a mouthful of that sweet savory delight. "You are good," she managed to get out, covering her mouth with her hand.

"Sorry for not doing more of this sooner. Maybe always," was Michael's reply. "It was difficult for me to see that working was not all there was to life. It didn't start out that way, and I never meant for it to get that way. When we were in college, somehow, I guess I thought we would be around each other all the time. We were then, but not so much anymore. But I promise you, it will never be that way again. There has to be another way, and we are going to find it. I want to live and work with you, side by side, every day. Manny was telling me the strangest thing today about his business."

"Manny? Manny the insurance guy that was in business with your father?" was Marie's slightly startled reply, pulling her head back and making a questioning smirk on her face.

"Yes, that's the one," was Michael's reluctant response, shrugging his shoulders. "Yeah, I know, he has always been all business and never 'talks shop' with anyone. But that's sort of my point. He was actually friendly today. Like he changed and really cared. Anyway, he gave me a couple books." Michael pointed to the books he left on the bedside stand. "He says he wants to spend more time with Elizabeth. He seemed sad talking about the past... a little emotional I guess you could say. He really sounds like he is going to change some things."

Marie shrugged, and took a sip from her glass, motioning to Michael to pour her another. "Okay, I guess. But what has that got to do with us again? You are losing me a little. Hum?" She said as she half swallowed a giggle. The champagne was definitely making her feel relaxed.

"Yeah, I get it. It's just that..." Michael took a sip from his glass, and paused staring at the bubbles and then smiling looking at Marie, "It's just that there has to be a way, some sort of a path to more of this," he said, motioning with his hand in a broad opening gesture referring to their voyage. "I remember that Jon guy that was a couple years behind us in school. He and his wife quit their jobs and are doing something working together. I don't even know if they go to an office. All I know is THEY go on vacation and THEY get to be at all their kids' events. That's what I want for us, too." Michael picked up the remote to turn on the surround sound stereo that he had already loaded with several of their favorite tunes. They laughed and talked for a while until they had almost finished off the champagne.

"Well, you are really full of surprises today, Michael Stoneman. But I want you to know, I don't care about before. I know you were doing all that for us. When I married you, I said it was for everything and forever. I meant it then and I mean it now and I will mean it tomorrow." Marie leaned forward to kiss Michael again, now beginning to feel the champagne a little. "Do you have any more surprises for me?" she smiled, playfully asking the question.

"As a matter of fact, Mrs. Stoneman, I do." Michael set the glass on the bench, got up, and went to one of the chests of drawers. He pulled out some type of garment and began taking off his shirt. "Close your eyes."

Marie closed her eyes. "This is my favorite part!"

"Okay, you can open them now." Marie was somewhat shocked by what she saw. Michael was standing where she could see him from head to foot. He was wearing a full-length night shirt. And it seemed to have writing on the front.

"A night shirt? Really?" Marie laughed. "Michael, you just love to play your little tricks on me!" She was smiling.

"Yes, but this time it is not a trick. I had to use a night shirt to get the whole poem I wrote you on the front." Michael tipped his head down and pointed to the lettering that covered the front of the night shirt. "See?"

As Marie now strained to look closer, she could see what Michael was saying. There on the front of the nightshirt was a handwritten poem entitled, "My Love" and signed at the bottom, "-from Michael to Marie." Marie got a little misty eyed. "When did you do this?" Marie asked.

"This afternoon. I got the idea and when I started to write, it just happened all at once. Would you like me to read it to you?"

Marie nodded her head. "Please."

Michael read the following words:

My Love

Some men search their whole lives
For an answer, but are unaware
That their wealth and power are nothing...
To my treasure those do not compare.
For I have found what was lost
That one needful missing part
When I found the love of my life
When she again stole my heart.

Some ride the waves of life
In search of the answer true
My voyage brought me the greatest joy
When I found my way to you.

So others can chase their fortunes
Lives spent in toil and strife
I choose to travel a different path
With my children and my wife.
And if we have great wealth
Or have no money at hand
We will have the true riches
For which we take a stand.

Some ride the waves of life
In search of any answer true
But the winds of life, love, and loyalty
These brought me home to you.

Gold and silver may elude
Fancy cars and clothes, too,
But I would trade every last possession,
For just one more moment with you.

Marie was crying as she reached out to embrace Michael. She kissed his neck and held him close. After a moment she was able to regain her composure and walked to the dresser to retrieve a Kleenex. Walking to one of the four candles, she blew it out. She was smiling.

"Michael, I love your poem. But there is something I think is missing," she said, blowing out the second candle, darkening the room even more.

"What's wrong with it?" Michael asked, trying to hide the pain in his voice.

Marie blew out the third candle, and now only one was left. "It is a beautiful work of art Michael. I think I would like my poem to be hung on the wall or a door or something." She had an impish grin on her face. Michael began to smile, too. Walking over to the closet door that had hooks for robes, Michael removed the poem and hung it on the hooks. As he turned to Marie, she blew out the last candle, and the room was pitch black.

"Well, my love, I hope we do not break any toes," was Michael's comment as he chuckled and took her hand. They carefully made their way to the oversized queen bed, but did not quite get there. Michael stumbled over one of his shoes. They tried to steady each other, but fell into the bed, laughing.

"Michael, you have such a romantic way about you," Marie teased as they tried to get under the covers in the dark.

"As long as it makes you happy, I'm good," was Michael's reply as he embraced her and gave her a long kiss.

The day that had started as a dream that changed their hearts forever, continued to unfold into an adventure. It was the adventure that became their love and their life together, heard of and longed for by many, but experienced only by the brave few that would dare to dream again, and dare to choose the winds of loyalty. We all choose.

CHAPTER 1:

THE DRIVE TO WORK

"I could do this drive in my sleep," Michael muttered under his breath to himself. "Like being on autopilot." He snickered to himself as he re-thought his comment, and then again muttered, "Or maybe a hamster on a wheel!" He shook his head at the thought, almost like a shudder.

It was a little darker out today than normal, but he was not going to let that get in his way. Today was a big day for Michael. Not because it was Friday, the last workday this week, but because it was the last day before he did something he had not done in years. He was going to take a vacation. Michael had not taken a vacation since he officially started the company just over five years ago.

"Okay, Michael, okay. Time to focus and get yourself together. You have a lot to do today, my man," he said in a low voice. This was Michael's usual morning "talk-to-me" routine. It was just his way of getting himself ready for the events of the day. Getting things in order. Getting things right in his head. "Let's see. Wrap up the Silverman project contract, call my mom to chat about the kids before we leave, e-mail my brother, sign off on the bonuses, recheck our flight's status, and meet briefly with Jimmy."

Jimmy was Michael's partner. They had grown up together. Same schools, same sports, even some of the same hobbies. They had pretty much become inseparable, especially after the accident. When Michael started his business, it only seemed right to have Jimmy there as his right-hand man. Who else could he trust Like Jimmy? Who else was as loyal? Besides, Jimmy was better at almost everything in school than him. About the only thing he ever beat Jimmy at was winning the affection of his wife. They both had serious crushes throughout their childhood on the same girl. But Michael won her heart, and they were married several years before Michael started the company. Jimmy always gave Michael a hard time about it. Jimmy said that she felt close to Michael because she had lost her parents just before high school and was raised by an older brother and his family. Michael would just smile. After all, he really owed Jimmy his life.

"Strange," Michael said to himself. "Seems a little darker out this morning, and quieter. Must be something changing in the air. Man, I hope we don't get a big storm and it delays the flight!" "Where was I? Oh yeah, let's see." Michael picked up his dictation recorder, hit record, and began to make verbal notes. "Verify that Silverman was basically satisfied with the proposal. Check the changes our team has made. Stop by to sign the contracts before you leave town. We get the contract on the software for their facility, with the annual maintenance contract. We own the software; they only license it. We can then repackage and resell to others as custom solutions for them. Lilly, make certain we place this on a schedule for upgrade and change every twelve months starting in month two." Always planning for the next sale.

"Call Mom and ensure her that everything will be alright. Everyone takes cruises. If she can help make the kids feel happy, life will be good. Oh yes, and about the dog. This morning my kids announced that mom is getting a dog at her house for them," he paused, thinking about his dog, Ransom, from when he was a kid. Or at least his mom had told him about the dog. "Mom, you need to think this dog thing through, okay? That is a lot of responsibility for you don't you think? If you want a pet, let me get you some fish or something." Michael felt like she should be thinking about a retirement community, and a dog would certainly interfere with his plans for that. Michael was relentless in focusing on how to close the deal.

His Mom was always afraid when Michael had to fly over or be near water. His dad had drowned when he was a kid. Michael and his dad were out with Jimmy and his dad on a fishing trip at the lake, just about this time of year. They were having a great time and then there was a loud thud. All Michael remembers was being thrown forward in the boat and hitting his head. The next thing he knew he was coming to on the sand bar with Jimmy leaning over him shouting his name. Jimmy's dad was a few feet away, laying on his side gasping for air. Michael's dad was nowhere around. His dad's body was pulled out of the river later that day, pretty messed up from the impact, and not far from the sandbar, from the hollow where they always caught the biggest fish. His mom never remarried; said she would always be comparing his dad to someone else. She became friends with Jimmy's dad, who eventually took to drinking. Guess he never got over that day.

"E-mail to John. Hey there brother, need to ask another favor. You know how Mom is about all this stuff. With her taking care of the kids and all, and now she's talking about getting a dog? Discourage that one, my brother. Can you look in on her like, I don't know, every day? We are going to be out of range on much of the cruise and you know how she gets about the whole water and cruise thing, especially this time of year. Just make sure she is good and enjoys the time with the kids. And, try to keep her from spending too much time around Robert. You know I love the guy, but his drinking gets worse this time of year. I don't want the kids to have to see too much of that with us gone," Michael recorded. Robert was Jimmy's dad. They were coming up on the anniversary of the accident, and it was really telling on his old man.

"Get the 50k cashier's check from the bank courier. Make certain to set up the transition. Work out the details of the redemption finalization. Meet with Jimmy. Congratulate him on moving him to Executive Vice President. Give him the bonus check. Arrange to sign redemption after we get back. And leave early!" Michael was not usually enthusiastic about time away from work. And given that it was going to interfere with the redemption, it really was not great timing. But the vacation package arranged by Jimmy's connection just made it too good to pass up. Jimmy was always looking out for him. You don't come across friends that stick by you through thick and thin like that every day.

"Michael, it looks like a storm, my man. Better call the travel company to confirm the flights," Michael said to himself. He picked up his phone from the seat next to him. "Strange," he thought to himself. "No signal?" he said out loud. "Must be the storm." Michael looked up just in time to hit the brakes. He had just pulled into the parking garage at work. "Wow! Talk about autopilot! I don't remember most of the drive let alone turning in here. I HAVE to get my head in the game. Must be the vacation thing throwing me off." He parked the car and got out. "The skies seemed to be, somehow, like glazed over or something", he thought to himself.

CHAPTER 2:

FIRST MEETING

L ooking at the high rise building that housed the offices of the company, Michael muttered to himself as he walked toward them, "Yes, this is definitely a cruise control day." He was so preoccupied with the events of the day leading up to his first vacation in... (well, he wasn't quite sure, but it had been more than five years) he couldn't even remember parking the car or the slow ride down in the "Elevator of Chance." The guys had fondly named the parking garage elevator in keeping with how they felt every time they stepped in for a ride. It was an elevator ride of many bumps and questionable safety. He didn't care about that. He didn't care about much; except he was about to be entering the building he knew only too well and starting the last day before VACATION!

Just another thirty paces or so, past the homeless guys looking for a handout, and the end begins. Normally Michael would race on by. He thought the whole handout thing was a scam. "They should just get jobs," he would always think to himself. But today was different. Today was HIS day and he really needed to get it completed to get on his way.

There was one old man that always seemed to stand out from the rest. Michael would usually drop his pocket change into his open bag in front of the seat he sat on. Today this old man seemed to stand out even more, in a strange kind of way. Wanting to seem generous, he dropped a twenty-dollar bill into his cup as he passed by. "Have to hurry," he thought to himself, moving briskly.

"They're all the same, Michael. They're all the same." It was the old man, and he was sort of muttering. But it was loud enough for Michael to hear. He turned back to the old man.

"What did you say?" Michael asked.

"What?" snapped the old man, defensively.

"Just now. You said my name, Michael. How did you know my name?" Michael inquired, feeling slightly agitated.

"So, did you like buy the sole rights to that name? You the only guy that can use it or what?" the old man quipped. Pausing slightly, he added, "Sheesh! Gimme a break over here!"

"Yeah, yeah," Michael countered. "But why today? I have been walking past you every day for five years and you say nothing."

"Exactly!" snapped the old man again.

"Now all of a sudden you say my name?" Michael would not let it go.

"What's with you and the name? You act you're the only one widt dat name!" the old man exclaimed, oddly adding an accent.

Fumbling through some papers he had pulled from his pocket as he stood up from his well-worn camping chair, he dropped what appeared to be money, a bill. Both he and Michael bent down at the same time to pick it up. Michael caught it as the wind was about to carry it away. It was a $100 bill. With what must have been an astonished look on his face as they both stood up, Michael extended his arm with the money in hand to return it. The old man nodded in acceptance and reached for the bill, exposing a very expensive watch on his arm. Michael knew just how expensive because he had one just like it, only the old man's was very old and worn. "Wow," Michael thought to himself, "Where did this old guy get the cash, and the cash for that watch?"

"You think you the only guy that ever made a dime?" the old man said indignantly as he snatched the bill from Michael's hand. The expression on Michael's face was telling, and it spoke very loudly what he was thinking. It was clear that Michael had decided a lot about the old man. It was clear that the old man did not like it.

"Why are you doing this?" Michael asked.

"Doing what?" the old man replied.

"Why are you doing this bum routine?" Michael said, expounding on his question.

"Why do you see me like a bum?" He quickly snapped back. "Look, I gotta get home." The old man struggled to pick up his backpack and the folding camping chair he had been sitting on. "Want to give me a hand over here?" he asked Michael.

"Hey look, I would love to help you, but I am late for a meeting?" said Michael, offering up a weak, half true excuse.

"Of course you would," replied the old man, shaking his head with just a trace of a smirk on his face.

"Look, the homeless shelter is all the way across town and..."

"Who said I live at the homeless shelter?" the old man said as he began folding up his camping chair.

"Well, you're here every day, and, well, you know, I just assumed..."

"Of course you did," said the old man, cutting Michael off again, which noticeably irritated Michael a little.

"Look, I help you every day and I have to go inside now..." Again, Michael did not get a chance to finish.

"Is that what you call it?" asked the old man, interrupting him. He had stopped collecting his things and stood up to look Michael in the eye.

"Call what?" asked Michael, puzzled.

"What you do every day. Help?" the old man responded.

"Well, you're the only one I give money to every day when I pass by," Michael offered as an explanation that even he began to now see as lacking.

"Right. When you pass by. Tell you what." The old man was on a bit of a roll now, realizing that Michael really did not care to help. "You just run along. Hurry up to your little meeting in your little office. I got this!"

With that he threw his camping chair over one shoulder and tugged at his backpack, dragging it. Unfortunately, in all their going back and forth, Michael ended up standing on a corner of it when he had stepped closer. As the old man tugged at it to walk away, Michael's foot stretched the worn and frayed fabric beyond its limits and caused the zipper to break. Flopping open, the backpack spilled out many composition notebooks. The old man got down on his hands and knees to begin picking them up and trying to get them back in the backpack. Michael was mortified at what he had done to this poor homeless man.

"I don't think this is quite how I thought my day would go," Michael thought to himself. "Nope, just not quite the day I had planned." He thought for the moment about his day. He thought about his lovely wife waiting for him to get off early. He thought about all of the tasks he had placed on his list. And he thought of what the old man had said to him. Was he really that self-absorbed? Hmm.

"Let me help," Michael said, getting down on his hands and knees to try to help the old man recover from the damage he had caused.

CHAPTER 3:

ASSUMPTIONS

– WHAT IS IT THEY SAY?

"I am really sorry," Michael told the old man as he bent down to help. For a single backpack, there seemed to be so many of these composition books. All of them were the plain black and white versions Michael remembered from college. Several seemed somewhat new. Others were old and well worn. Among this pile of the well-worn he noticed one titled, "The Beautiful Marie."

"'The Beautiful Marie'. Hmm. That's my wife's name," Michael said, half thinking out loud and half trying to break the clumsy silence. He was still feeling the impact of his accidental damage to the old man's property.

"Let me guess," the old man glibly replied. "You bought that name too!"

"No, no. Just made me think of her is all." Michael was moved by thoughts of his wife. Flashes of their lives together quickly raced through his mind. Her understanding words, his many broken promises of not working so much. Finally, this vacation would help to change all that. And all of that in just a fleeting few seconds. "I say that to her sometimes." Michael was just about completed with the task of collecting the books that had been strewn about when the zipper broke. "She really is an amazing woman. An amazing person." There was something about his wife's name and helping the old guy. It was odd. It, well, it felt good.

"Hadn't you better stop messing with my stuff and get off to your little meeting?" the old man asked, reaching out and taking the books from Michael's hands.

"I don't really have a meeting," Michael admitted, a bit sheepishly.

"Oh?" the old man replied, not looking up as he focused on getting far too many notebooks back into his damaged backpack.

"Yeah, I was just saying that so you would stop talking and I could go." As he said the words, Michael wondered a bit at his own candor on the subject. Strange. There was just something about the old man that was... familiar, or disarming, or comforting, in spite of his abrupt nature. Strange.

"So, go already! I ain't no invalid." The old man responded in a tone that sounded almost as if he were testing Michael's true willingness to help him.

"No, that's okay. Not much happening there today anyway." Perhaps there was a little sarcasm showing through in his voice because the old man stopped what he was doing and looked up. "Wow," thought Michael to himself. "His eyes look like they are looking right through me." "Besides, I really don't take much time away from the office. It will be fine," Michael continued.

"What are you doing now?" asked the old man as Michael got out his phone to reach out to the office.

"I am texting my partner to let him know I will be taking a couple hours off this morning for personal business," Michael responded. "That should be enough time to help get you to the Homeless Shelter. Marie would want me to do that."

"Hah!" the old man snickered, shaking his head as he put the finishing touches on the repacked bag.

"What?" inquired Michael, almost a little hurt by what seemed like the old man shunning his assistance.

"You and that Homeless Shelter thing you got going on," said the old man, shaking his head as he applied some safety pins to the opening in the backpack left by the broken zipper. Bzz-Bzz. Michael's phone went off and he read the text, not really hearing the old man. "What's it say?" the old man asked.

"My partner said he is marking this day on the calendar. Says it is about time I took some personal time off when I want to, without one of my big plans. And I guess my assistant already told everyone I was not coming in today." Michael smiled as he shook his head, thinking of how his assistant was always looking out for him. "Taxi! Taxi!"

"What are you doing?" the old man asked with a puzzled look on his face.

"Getting a taxi," Michael replied without looking back at the old man, preoccupied with trying to wave down one of the yellow chariots that normally overwhelmed the city streets.

"It's about twenty-eight blocks from here, right?"

"You mean the Homeless Shelter?" the old man inquired with his head tilted to the side in a thoughtful, confused manner.

"Yes," said Michael, trying to waive down the next yellow streak.

"Yes, yes it is," said the old man shaking his head and looking at his feet.

"Taxi! Taxi!" Michael had stepped off the curb, half by accident and half on purpose, and into the path of one of these steaming yellow monsters on its relentless pursuit of transportation and commerce. In a moment Michael knew that the taxi was not going to be able to stop. Suddenly he felt a large hand grab the back collar of his jacket. With a strong jerking motion, it whisked him to safety just before what likely would have been a fatal meeting with a taxi front bumper. Michael looked back over his shoulder expecting to see the old man immediately behind him. The street was pretty much empty of other pedestrians. Oddly the old man was still on the far side of the sidewalk, smiling. There was no one else around that could have pulled Michael to safety. Michael's forehead wrinkled together a bit. His mind was half in that inquisitive moment that comes from not being able to believe what we see, and half in a borderline outrage at the long since gone taxi driver. "What's up with these taxi drivers?! Taxi! Taxi! It's like worse than ignoring me. It's like they don't even see me. Taxi! Taxi!" Michael was becoming noticeably frustrated at what he thought was unjust treatment, possibly because he was with the homeless guy.

"Maybe they are just smarter than you," the old man said, smiling.

"What are you talking about?" Michael asked. Still not looking at the old man he was frantically waving his arms back and forth over his head, and even whistling with his fingers in his teeth, to get the attention of any taxi he could.

"I don't live twenty-eight blocks away," the old man replied still smiling.

"But the Homeless Shelter..." Michael had turned and made eye contact with the old man now.

"Kid, obviously you are not a brain surgeon. I don't live at the Homeless Shelter," said the old man with a steel like quality in his voice.

Michael stopped and turned to the old man. He cocked his head sideways and backwards at the same time, like a bobble-head in disbelief. He had that inquisitive wrinkle on his forehead. "Where do you live?" asked Michael.

Chapter 4:

The Journey Home

The old man just shook his head and looked at the ground.

"No, seriously, where do you live?" Michael pressed for an answer.

"Just a couple blocks away," responded the old man, with a bit of annoyed impatience in his voice. "Here, grab that stack," he said, handing a large stack of the notebooks to Michael to carry.

"How did all these notebooks fit in that bag with the others he already put in there?" Michael thought to himself. He struggled a little, almost lost the unbalanced load, and then regained his equilibrium, getting the stack under control.

"C'mon. It's this way," said the old man gesturing with the hand that was holding the tattered camping chair, already half turned in the same direction. He began walking.

"Okay," replied Michael. He took a couple quick steps to get side by side with the old man. Michael still struggled a bit under the load of his shoulder strapped brief case that carried his computer and other work items while balancing the steno books.

"So, what is it you do in your little office?" the old man asked, trying to make polite small talk as they walked.

"My work involves IT," said Michael in what was a small part of the beginning of his well-rehearsed elevator speech. He didn't get far with it.

"You a manager or just a mail room guy, or what?" the old man asked interrupting Michaels little monologue.

Michael looked away from the old man to the ground in front of him. He was hoping to do a better job of navigating the cracks in the sidewalk so as not to repeat his misstep that caused all of the notebooks to hit the ground earlier. Although he wasn't used to carrying them, and he was a little clumsy at it, he was surprised at how light they were. It was almost as if they weighed nothing at all. "Of course," Michael thought to himself, "I did work out once this month." Grinning at the thought that the old man did not realize he was the major owner of the company, he replied, "Well, yes, I guess you could say I am a manager." "This old guy probably doesn't know anything about computers, like a lot of people his age," Michael continued thinking to himself.

There was a moment of silence while they waited for the streetlight to indicate they could cross. What was normally a very busy street, this morning was noticeably calmer than normal. "I see," said the old man, again trying to be cordial. Making it to the other side, they began their journey again. They were walking down another sparsely pedestrian-populated sidewalk, also unusual for this area this time of day. "So, just how many its do you manage?" the old man asked, seemingly trying to make informed conversation.

"No, no," replied Michael, smiling as much on the inside as he was on the outside. He must have been right about the old man and computers. "Not it. IT is short for Information Technology."

The old man stopped and looked at Michael. "You always this slow?" he chided Michael, and started walking again.

"Why? Am I not keeping up? Are you in a hurry? Do we need to walk faster?" Michael was a little confused by the comment and now trying to focus on the task of getting to the old man's house.

"I wasn't talking about walking," said the old man. "I was talking about thinking," he said, half shaking his head while shrugging his shoulders.

"Oh. You were just messing with me. I got it," Michael said with a sheepish voice a little embarrassed at the assumptions now that he had made about the old man. "I guess this old guy knows a lot more than I imagined," Michael thought to himself, and it showed on his face.

"Right," said the old man with an air of sarcasm in his voice.

They turned at a very small, run down old house, with overgrown shrubs and a spotty lawn. It was only a few steps up the uneven concrete walk as they stepped onto the weather-beaten wood porch. Michael took care as he stepped toward the door. He was a little concerned about the stability of the porch, given its current condition.

"Did we really just walk two city blocks that fast? Why, it must have been your great conversational skills were just a bit to stimulating for me to notice," Michael said, beaming. He was trying to match the old man's wit, trying to "catch up."

The old man looked up from his keys with a slight wide-eyed start. Then, his mouth turned up a bit at the corners in the closest thing to a smile Michael had seen on the old man's face in five years. He might have even chuckled as he nodded his head, looked back to select the correct key, and slipped it in the lock. Unlocking the door, he opened it. Stepping in, he gestured for Michael to follow, just as he disappeared into the inner room.

Michael followed and struggled with his load as he shut the door behind him. He was intent on not dropping anything as his eyes adjusted to the light. Turning around he expected to find an empty table for the old man's belongings. Michael was stunned at what saw. His jaw dropped open slightly.

Chapter 5:

Room For Living

"Hey, kid, you're gonna catch flies like that." the old man commented to Michael, seeing his mouth open from surprise. Michael, momentarily stunned by the view, snapped free from his awe-struck state to catch a glimpse of the old man. Was that a smile? Odd. It was as if the old man had somehow changed now that he was back in his own home. "Must be the familiar environment," Michael thought to himself.

The old man was clearly enjoying the moment. Smiling from ear to ear, he asked, "Want some tea? Maybe coffee?"

"Either one," Michael replied, still somewhat captivated by what he saw there on the wall in front of him. The old man stepped into what he assumed was a very small kitchen (more like a closet) to make the dark brew. The house did not look large from outside, but somehow, he thought is was bigger than what was before him. "It must extend past these rooms," he thought to himself.

"Coffee it is then," he heard the old man reply, amid the sounds of clinking coffee pot and running water. Michael did most of a 360 to drink in the view. Amazing!

Michael was standing in a small living room, or what he assumed was meant to serve as a living room. "What was this space, maybe 10x10, 10x12 tops?" he pondered to himself. "And, wow, the shelves." There was a two-seat couch and a small overstuffed chair. A modest brass floor lamp and end table separated them. A rectangular (just barely, it was so small) coffee table was squarely positioned in front. And the TV..., well, among other things, it was the smallest flat screen TV he had ever seen – maybe 22 inches? And if the screen size wasn't small enough, the old man had shoved some pictures of people, animals, whatever, between the screen and the plastic frame all the way around. There were so many photos that there was hardly any screen to speak of showing to see what might actually be playing. But that was not the most striking view in the room.

On every wall, almost from floor to ceiling, were those workshop like rail and channel do-it-yourself wall mounted bookshelves. And these were not your ordinary bookshelves. There was nothing ordinary about the old man so far, so why should the bookshelves be different? No, these shelves were not filled with the classics, or National Geographic collections of magazines, or Readers' Digests. There were none of those artsy-fartsy coffee table books of Van Gogh and others that just collect dust and are collected to look good to guests. No, these bookshelves were almost completely filled with rows (and sometimes strewn with stacks) of what looked like..., yes, they were filled with more composition notebooks. Most of them looked quite worn, and still others were in the clear 2-for-1 sale wrappers. "This dude REALLY needs to get out more!" Michael thought to himself.

"Nice TV," Michael called over his shoulder in the direction of the kitchenette. His comment dripped with sarcasm. Yet, this old man was starting to intrigue him. Not that he reached out to others often, but maybe he could help the old guy escape this, this... whatever. "What is your favorite show?"

"The one that's playing now," quipped back the old man, ignoring the sarcastic tone that showed only slightly in Michael's words. Michael walked from left to right, scanning the plethora of what he thought was literary nothingness. He made his way to the corner where the TV stood out from the shelves. That's when he noticed the TV was unplugged. He shook his head as he picked up the end of the cord in his hand, noticing that is was a little frayed and had one tong so badly bent that there was no way it could be used. "Dude. Dude. Dude," Michael thought to himself about the old man as he continued to shake his head.

"So..., you must be a writer then?" Michael commented in a statement like question, still talking over his shoulder.

""What makes you say that?" came the old man's voice amidst the familiar sound of coffee brewing in a cheap K-Mart special coffee maker that the old man had forever. And the coffee, ahhh, the aroma. It was outstanding!

"I didn't. Your walls did," Michael responded. He was still scanning the shelves and twirling the frayed cord between his thumb and forefinger.

"They are just thoughts, Michael. They are just thoughts," the old man replied.

"By the looks of things," said Michael, "You have been thinking a lot!" Michael dropped the cord and strolled back along the shelves. This time he was trying to catch a glimpse of anything that might give away the contents of any of the notebooks. That's when he noticed a space in the middle shelf about half-way between the ends.

"The great thing is, at my age, I keep finding brand new stories in these books." You could almost hear the old man's grin in his voice as he continued the conversation from his brewing station in the kitchenette.

"I get it. It's a joke about old age," said Michael shaking his head a bit at the corny response from the old man. He was intrigued by the blank space in the shelves and wanted to investigate it but began to notice some of the hand-written titles scribbled on some of the notebooks. "When "E" does not equal mc², "My thoughts on quantum mechanics", "Love, Life, and Loyalty". "Who is this guy, and who spends time writing this much stuff on so many different topics?" Michael thought to himself. He also saw what looked like half-a-dozen or more titles that looked like ethnic recipe books. "And by hand?"

"I am glad to see you are starting to catch up. Any simpler and I would have to say, 'Pull my finger' to get you to smile." The old man's tone was clearly facetious, but somehow, Michael appreciated his humor. "Black or cream and sugar?" came the voice from the kitchen.

"Black with artificial sweetener, if you have it," Michael replied. "Thanks."

The old man emerged from the tiny kitchen/dinette carrying a small serving tray. On it were two plain dull off-white heavy ceramic coffee mugs filled with the darkest of steaming black coffees Michael had seen. And the aroma was so luscious that one could almost eat the mist coming off the cups. There on the tray was a small plate with a handful of those cheap raspberry centered sugary cookies. Michael recognized them because they were one of his favorites, and his wife wouldn't let him get them anymore. She was trying to get him to set an example for the children of being healthier by improving his eating habits. Secretly, he bought these on a regular basis and kept them in a drawer in his office. Yes, he knew them well. The old man set the tray on the end table between the couch and chair, then took a seat in the chair that seemed a little small for him. The whole setting was Hobbit-like.

"Here's your coffee," the old man said, beaming with pride in being able to offer something to a guest. "Please, sit down and take a load off." He gestured toward the couch for Michael to take a seat. "Take a moment to enjoy your coffee before you have to head back."

"Thank you," replied Michael in his well-practiced polite voice. "So, you said you had to get home. I thought maybe you had some TV show to watch or something. But I see that's not the case," he said, pointing to the now exposed inoperable cord on the television. "What was your hurry, if you don't mind my asking?" As soon as the words were out of his mouth, Michael found himself surprised at what he was saying. He had known this guy what, thirty minutes, and he was sitting in his strange little house drinking coffee he did not see him make and asking him personal questions about his life?!? Somehow, the old man made him feel comfortable, like they were good friends or something. But then he had seen him almost every day for five years, even if only in passing. That must be it. Besides, he was very intrigued by it all, in some way.

"No, I don't mind you asking, if you don't mind the answer," the old man replied with a gentle look of wisdom on his face and a steady voice that had almost a velvet quality. This was very different from the voice that had been giving him such a hard time less than an hour ago.

"What do you mean?" Michael asked, growing more curious by the moment of the old man's words and the sound of that voice. He took a sip of what he thought was the most delicious coffee that had ever passed between his lips, and he considered himself a connoisseur of fine coffees. Michael preferred making his own at home, to even the best of the offerings of the franchised coffee cathedrals.

"Well, sometimes my stories make people uneasy. I would be happy to explain, though, if you really want to know. But it is not a short answer. Do you have some time?" the old man replied with a question that somehow had that different ring to it, that velvet-like quality. It was like it was in 3D or something, standing out from the conversation.

"Yeah, I didn't think it would be," Michael responded. "I have time." This time it was his own voice that had a slightly peculiar ring to it. "I hope this old guy didn't slip me a Mickey," Michael thought to himself as the old man continued.

CHAPTER 6:

THE STORYTELLER

"Okay," nodded the old man in response to Michael's request. "You may have to get out your little Dick Tracy communicator and let your boss know you will be later than you thought today." The old man grinned as he returned to that familiar sarcastic chiding voice.

"Yeah, actually I was thinking I might just take his advice and take the day off," Michael nodded, taking another sip of the what must be the old man's special brew. "And he is NOT my boss. He is my partner. And technically, since I own most of the company, I am the boss." Again, Michael felt a little odd at sharing so much information, but he was becoming increasingly more comfortable with the old man and his company. He even began to find some humor in the sarcastic retorts.

"Of course he's not. Of course you are," nodded the old man grinning and drinking his coffee. "Anyone could see you are completely in charge. The man at the wheel. The captain of the ship. I see." There was that velvet voice again.

"My wife – Marie – wanted some help with stuff around the house today anyway. I can go help her when we finish." Michael was talking and at the same time texting his partner Jimmy that he was taking the day off. "Bzz." "Bzz." Jimmy's reply was "Great! You need the time off. We can take care of our paperwork stuff when you get back. Have a great vacation!" (He took another sip from his coffee. Sitting back, he relaxed on the couch. Michael looked the old man in the eyes that seemed gently fiercened over time.) In a half-request, half-directive tone, Michael asked "So, go ahead, tell me, why the rush home?"

The old man again sipped his coffee, looking Michael in the eye. Then, setting the coffee on the tray and picking up one of the cookies, he motioned to Michael to do the same. He did.

"Why does anyone hurry, Michael?" the old man asked as he began the story. Michael shrugged and shook his head slightly as he took a bite of the familiar tasting treat. He wasn't sure of the desired answer to the question. "Because they want to get somewhere sooner rather than later," the old man continued, answering his own question. "It's about the 'want to'. It's about what's important, right?"

Michael nodded, enjoying another cookie which he now dunked in the aromatic coffee.

"So, what's important to you?" the old man asked. And there was that velvet quality in the questioning voice.

"I thought you were going to tell me about you?" Michael asked, slightly repositioning himself in his seat. He was quite caught off guard by the question. Frankly, it made him feel a little uncomfortable.

"I am," came the old man's quick reply. Michael looked puzzled. "I told you sometimes my stories make people uneasy. What I am saying is you will get what I am saying better if I compare it to something important to you. Make sense?"

Michael nodded. "Yeah, okay. Well, there's my job. And there's my family of course, and the stuff we do together like cook outs or church or soccer games or school plays. And there's our friends. Stuff like that."

"Hmm," the old man was nodding. "I see. Sounds a lot like my list when I was your age. I guess a lot like lists many people think they have. I have seen you almost every day for the last five years on your way to work. Just watching you scurrying into that building while you check the time on your expensive watch so you can be at least five minutes early tells me just how important work is to you. But what about the other stuff you mentioned?"

"What do you mean?" Michael asked in a puzzled voice.

"You might say that I am like a witness to how important work is to you. Tell me, who is a witness to how important that other stuff is to you? How would anyone know?" came the old man's question in that velvet voice.

"Marie knows," Michael retorted in an almost snapping defensive posture to the somewhat too personal, probing question. "She knows that I work like I do for her and the family. When my daughter wanted some dancing lessons so she could be in the school plays we were able to get her into the best dance school. My son was able to get the top of the line soccer shoes for soccer so he could play his best, even if I couldn't be there for all the games. I give to the church, even when I can't make the services. I just go online and hit the "Giving" button. A couple years ago I bought nice Bibles for all of us. And my wife and I are about to go on our first vacation in years. People know."

"I see," replied the old man thoughtfully, stroking his chin. "So, what do you think is important to me?"

Chapter 7:

The Story Unfolds

"Well," said Michael, looking around, "Looks like writing in these little books has got to be in your Top 10." Michael got up and side stepped the too small coffee table, moving to the bookshelf again. With coffee in hand he strolled again down the length of the shelf, noticing not only the notebooks but this time seeing that there were more than a few regular books on the shelves. He pulled some out a bit here and there to look at the titles. "It's okay if I look, right?" he inquired.

"Sure. And they are important to me, but they are just thoughts," replied the old man, finishing the last of his coffee.

"Why do you have these classics like *Catcher in the Rye* and *Sleeping Beauty* mixed in with one's I never heard before like, *Van Gogh in Love* and *Watermarked* and these others?" posed Michael, tilting his head to see the titles from the notebooks as well.

"Because, Michael, the books I choose to read are all classics to me," came the old man's velvet reply.

"Hmm," Michael grunted, obviously pondering something.

"What?" asked the old man.

"I was just thinking," Michael replied in a bit wistful melancholy tone. "Many years ago, when I was a kid, I wanted to be a writer."

"And?" probed the old man.

"Well, you know," sighed Michael. "life changes things."

"Yes, I do know. I didn't always write either," said the old man, getting up from his Hobbit chair.

"What changed?" Michael, with renewed curiosity, replied.

"Well, now we are getting to it, to me. Let me tell you what changed. Quite a bit actually. But first, bring that box on the middle shelf there," the old man motioned, "and set it on the coffee table. I will warm up our coffee." The old man headed to the kitchen to retrieve the coffee urn and condiments.

Box in the middle? Michael did not see any box in the middle before... oh, wait. The space in the middle shelf. He bent down to look closer. Sure enough there was a box alright, more like an oversized jewelry chest or something. Actually, it looked a little like the pirates' chest from the movie he once saw, *Treasure Island*. He reached in, and grabbing it by the ornate handles, he pulled it from the shelf. Somehow it seemed bigger once he got it off the shelf. "Must be an optical illusion," he thought to himself, struggling with the load. It was heavier than he had anticipated. Moving awkwardly, he turned and placed it on the coffee table. "What's in it?" Michael asked, then in more of an exclamation he continued, "Bricks!?" He returned to his seat on the mini couch.

The old man was returning with the coffee urn and a dish with the sweetener. Setting them on the end table, he sat down and responded with a half-smile. "Close," he said. "Some things are heavier than others." Reaching into his pants pocket he retrieved an art nouveau style skeleton key, he placed it in the lock, gave it a quick turn that popped open the built-in lock, and returned the key to his pocket. "I first made this box when I was a kid. It was just sort of rectangular then. But over the years I kept adding to it and making it more ornate." He lifted the hasp, and then swung the top open to the back, revealing a luminescent interior. Michael would never have guessed the inside was so beautiful, judging from the outside.

The old man began to retrieve some of the contents – bits of paper, tattered from age. There were different sizes, and even some recipe cards or something like that. Michael was very intrigued at what the old man had collected to place in such an ornate box.

The old man leaned back in his chair. Picking up his coffee cup he brought it to just in front of his mouth. He steadied it with both hands while blowing gently across the top to cool it. From looking into the cup, to looking out the lace-curtain-clad front window on the same wall as the front door, the old man was momentarily silent. He was not looking at anything, just that intentional stare of remembrance while he briefly gathered his thoughts. Steadying his coffee mug with both hands, he took a sip, looked back into the cup, and then placed it back on the serving tray.

"Change is an interesting thing, Michael," the old man began. "It means you go from something to something. To tell you what changed I have to tell you about what once was true to what became true today. Like I said, it takes a while." The old man picked up his coffee cup and held it in both hands. It was as if there was a certain security in holding it; it was as if the story somehow flowed from this holding of the cup. He continued. "There was a time when I thought I had it all. Then I lost what I had – my wife, my kids, my business, my friends – everything." He stopped for a moment, looked at his coffee, then looked back at Michael. "When we were talking about what was important to you, I *said* your list sounded much like mine when I was younger."

"It's difficult to know where to start. You mentioned the vacation you are going to take. When I think about my life, in a way it was a vacation that turned things for the worse for me. Hopefully yours turns out better than mine did." He took a sip of coffee. "I learned a lot from that vacation, and what came after. Even things about when I was a kid."

Michael looked at him with confusion on his face. "How do you mean?"

The old man pulled what looked like a 3x5 card from the chest. It looked like a recipe card. At the top was scribbled "Hole in the Middle." "We were going to take a vacation. My mom always wanted our family to go across country on... like a camping trip or something. She never told me about it until the day my wife and I were going to leave on vacation. As a kid we never had the money, and my dad died before we could take the trip. It's a bit jumbled for me now. She told me some story about a family dog we had that saved me from getting hit by a delivery driver. The dog pushed me out of the way and got hit instead, right in our driveway. I don't remember it, but I guess the dog died the next day. I was very little she said. Anyway, my mom was always there for me. This was a recipe for a special breakfast she always made me as a kid. I never even knew what it was called until I saw this recipe card. I keep it to remind me of all of the good things she did for me, of my childhood when my dad worked a lot, and of how important my parents were to me. I hold this card, close my eyes, and remember how important those days were to me in my life". The old man's eyes were closed, and he was silent for a moment, and it was as if Michael could "see" his memories.

"Sure. Okay, I can see that you see that as an important part of your childhood, but you are kind of losing me here," Michael said, shaking off the 'visions' in his head of the old man's memories, a little uncomfortable with the old man's story. "I am missing the connection to what we were talking about – hurrying home, why you started writing... that is what we were talking about, right?"

The old man opened his eyes, clearly displaying a smile on his normally stoic face. A very peaceful, warm smile, as he spoke, "Yes. Yes. You are quite right." The old man again, reached into the chest and drew out what looked like tickets to events of some sort. He was smiling again as he broke the silence. "These are tickets to my daughter's plays and my son's soccer and football games. One of each of them, at least. I found these in my mother's belongings after she passed. The two adult tickets with the stubs gone were her and my wife. The child's ticket with the stub gone would be either my daughter or son because they went to each other's events."

"There is another adult ticket with the stub still attached. Did she buy an extra for, like a memento for a scrap book or something?" Michael asked.

"Well, that's how it turned out, but no, that is not why she bought them," The old man replied. He seemed to be getting a bit emotional as he continued. "Those were my tickets. I did not make it. I was busy working or on a road trip or something. To tell you the truth, I don't know why I missed these. When I looked through what my mother had saved, there were quite a few like this that I..." He stopped talking. His eyes were closed and there were small, ever so small, drops of moisture at the corners of his eyes.

"Yeah, okay. I totally understand. You had to provide, and you had to work. I understand that for sure," Michael said, trying to make the old man feel better.

"Right. Right," came the old man's reply as he opened his eyes. He cleared his throat, set the tickets down, and took a sip of his coffee. "I keep these to remind me of how important my own family is to me."

Michael was now noticeably fidgeting in his seat. He took a sip of coffee, looked at his watch, and set his cup down. "Please don't take this wrong. I get that these are important memories to you, but I am still not clear about the connection to why you wanted to hurry home and the writing thing." He noticed the old man sort of winced at the words he had spoken. He felt like a jerk. "So, you say this was in your mother's stuff when she passed. I am sorry to hear that. Has she been gone long?" Michael had switched to part-human, part-salesman mode, and was trying to make the old man feel better. He was trying to make himself feel better for being so insensitive about the old man's feelings.

"Well, it sometimes seems like just yesterday, and other days it seems like an eternity," came the old man's reply, a little stronger after another sip of coffee. He refilled Michael's cup from the urn, and then his own. "It's been a few years. She passed away tragically while we were on that vacation I mentioned." He took one of the cookies and dipped it in his coffee to soften it before taking a small bite.

"Wow, I am very sorry to hear that. I can see why you say you hope my vacation goes better than yours, having to cut it short and come back to that funeral." Michael was shaking his head. He picked up a cookie and followed suit with the old man.

"It's actually a bit more complicated than that," the old man said, reaching into the box and pulling out what looked like a restaurant receipt. There was nothing special about it that Michael could see, just a standard greasy spoon green and white ticket. The word "RECEIPT" in all caps and red printed at the top, like just about every diner in America has. And of course, there was some writing from the order on it, being a used receipt. But by now he knew it, too, would have its own story. The old man continued.

"My mother, God rest her soul, she was such a good lady, a good human being... a saint. She was always worried about everyone else, and it got even more so after my dad was gone. Always took in the limping stray dog and nursed it back to life, found it a home, and made sure the new owners had food for it. Same with cats. Once she found a bird with a broken wing in her yard and spent $500 of money she couldn't afford to spend at the vet to get it reset. She nursed that bird along the whole summer so that its wing would be strong enough to migrate. And she was the same with humans." Again, Michael could "see" the animals in his mind that the old man described. Although he could not explain it, it was as if the old man's velvety words became a "movie in his head", captivating him.

The old man leaned back in his chair now. Holding his heavy cup with both hands, he stared for a moment into it as if the answer would be there in the cup, then looked up to continue. "There was this old guy in town that she and my dad had known since they were kids. After my dad passed this old guy fell onto some hard times. He sort of became the town drunk. His son had money so he had what he needed in the way of a tiny apartment and his retirement money helped too. Not that his son ever spent any time with him. I guess that is why my mother felt bad for him, partly, him being all alone most of the time and all. Some of the details are not real clear because I had to put the story together from bits and pieces, including a recording she had made of a conversation she had with this guy just before she died." The old man leaned forward, set his cup on the tray, picked up the receipt, and stood up to walk toward the front window just a few feet away on the other side of the too small coffee table. Michael followed his every move with intensity. He hoped he had not somehow disturbed the old man with his questions. The old man stood there at the front window, looking out through the dusty lace curtains with his arms folded. Finally, after what seemed like forever (but was only really a minute or two) the old man spoke again.

"Apparently two days after we left, she got yet another of those daily calls from the town drunk. He kept asking her to meet, but we had taken the kids to her house on my last day of work instead of to my brothers for the first few days of our vacation like we planned because my wife was running late for her job. My mother told him she couldn't do it because she had the kids. Anyway, he wanted to meet her at one of her favorite little diners for coffee. And she was always trying to get him to eat something. Cherry pie." said the old man, waving the receipt slightly. "He claimed he had something to tell her, so she went to meet him there. She had been on the phone with my brother. Mom had been watching the kids but had taken them to his house so they could play with his kids. She told him where she was going and why. He tried to get her to just come back and go to lunch with the family, but she insisted that everyone needs someone to listen to them, and she would be over right after they were done. That was the last he heard from her. She never made it to his house. It seems in putting her phone away as she sat down, she turned on the recorder on her phone by accident as she put it in her purse, which made the recording muffled. The town drunk had something that had been weighing on him for years. He told her a disturbing story about how my dad had died that was different from what she had been told at the time. Not that he was murdered or anything. But apparently my old man was a hero." The old man looked down at the receipt, and two tears were going down his cheeks, one on each side. "The story disturbed her so much that she was determined to get to the bottom of it. She picked up this check, left more than enough cash on the table for the bill and tip, and headed out the door. She was so flustered that as she was looking in her purse – maybe for her phone to call my brother, maybe for her keys, or maybe to put this receipt in there where they found it later – she wasn't paying attention. She just quickly stepped off the curb to cross the street to her car, right in front of the city bus. She was conscious when they took her to the hospital. My brother and his family and my kids all got to see her. They said she really did not look that bad, but there was some internal bleeding the doctors could not stop. She died that night." He quickly wiped his cheeks and returned to his seat to take a sip of coffee. "If things had gone differently, if my wife had not been late, if I had been there, she would have called me and

I would have stopped in because it would have been on my way to work that morning from a business meeting I had in another part of town. My wife and I were really torn apart by the what-ifs, whose fault it is, all that. My wife lost her parents when she was young, so my mom was like a mom to her, too."

"I am so sorry. I did not mean to bring that up. I am really sorry," Michael repeated, this time with truly genuine heart-felt concern.

"No, no, it's okay. It's okay," said the old man waiving with one hand as if to calm Michael. "I keep this receipt for a couple reasons. First, it reminds me to think of the needs of others, even the need for me to listen to their stories. Her last act of her life was to think of others as important as herself. Secondly, because it was the last thing she ever held in her hand. You see, we took one of those secluded cruises where you don't get reception for most of the trip. It was a "special deal" arranged by ... by a friend. By the time we got back home, she was already buried. This is all I have to remember her last day."

"I can see why you said a vacation was the beginning of hard times," Michael commented clumsily. He really was not the type to get to emotionally wrapped up in others' lives, but this story was exceptional.

"That's only the beginning, Michael. That's only the beginning," the old man said, rubbing his chin. He stood up to head to the kitchen with the now empty cookie plate. "I'll be right back."

CHAPTER 8:

BETRAYAL AND INTRIGUE

After just a few minutes, the old man returned with two small salad plates, each with what looked like a sandwich cut in half. There was something yellow in between. "Egg salad," the old man said handing one plate to Michael. "You have to eat something."

Michael smiled. "I don't think I have had one of these since I was a kid. My mom made them for us when we would go to the pool for picnics," he said taking a bite.

The old man sat down again, taking a bite from his sandwich and returning it to the plate. He set his plate on the end table, wiped his mouth with a paper towel napkin, and again refreshed their coffees from the urn. Then he continued.

"Let me try to get through the rest of this. I have already taken up too much of your time, and you will need to be moving on soon," the old man said.

"It's okay," Michael responded between bites of his childhood dream sandwich. "I want to hear this. And this sandwich is great, by the way."

The old man smiled. "Yeah, sometimes simpler is better," as he too spoke between bites and nodded. He reached into the chest and retrieved some papers that were stuck together with a paperclip. Two tickets and a flyer from the cruise, and a much older flyer of an RV. "Anyway, I still remember what my wife said that morning as I went off to work the last day before our vacation. 'Maybe we'll meet some nice people on the trip and make some new friends.' She was partially right. We did meet some people. I guess they had even emailed her while I was at work because they saw our information on the passenger list, and we lived only about thirty minutes away. They were leaving from a different airport, so we did not actually meet them until we sailed. Donny and Carla seemed nice enough, alright. We had dinner with them the second night on the trip, did a few of the onboard events with them through the week, and went to the end-of-cruise bash the last night of the cruise. By then we had gotten to know each other pretty well, as well as you can in a few days. Donny was in sales and traveled a lot. Carla worked from home doing computer work. That night we were having dinner and my wife had sprained her ankle so when dinner was over, Carla asked me to dance. I looked at my wife and she told me to go ahead. Donny said they would just sit at the bar at the edge of the dance floor and chat. While Carla and I danced I noticed that my wife was doing most of the talking, and Donny listened attentively. Every once in a while, he would say something that would make her laugh. Carla and I would take a break to go and sit with them to chat. But that Carla, she really liked to dance. It seemed like my wife enjoyed talking with

Donny. I could tell because she would actually stop to let him talk, while she listened. When she and I talked, she talked at me, not with me. I remember seeing that from the dance floor. I guess it bothered me a little." The old man was doing the stare out the front window again. He paused, and in that stare, Michael somehow again could see what the old man was now reliving through the pain in his eyes.

"My wife was getting a little tired and a little bored sitting around. But Carla wanted to dance one more dance. Donny volunteered to take my wife up to the casino deck where we all were headed to walk around and maybe play some slots or blackjack or something. She said that sounded great, so they left the ballroom arm in arm to head that way. And I guess that bothered me a little as well. So, Carla and I had our last dance and decided to take a stroll on the deck to cool off for a minute before heading up to the casino. That turned out to be a bad choice," the old man said as he shuffled his feet and looked down at them, then back out the window. He continued.

"As we were walking around this one narrower bend in the deck, we stopped to take a last look at the ocean at night. There was a little shift in the ship and Carla fell back towards me and I caught her. As she regained her footing, she turned around and her face was very near mine. Slightly closing her eyes, she tilted her head and gave me a quick little kiss. I was startled, but it felt good, and I looked into her eyes. She leaned forward and kissed me very deeply. We were alone on the deck and she, well, she got very friendly for a few minutes. I finally came to my senses and pulled back and said, 'Might be good to head up to the casino.' She just smiled and said, 'Yeah. Who knows? We might get lucky!' At that point I was feeling very guilty and had already turned to walk to the elevator with her by my side. We made it up to the casino fine, and we both played it off like nothing had happened. But the guilt weighed heavy on me the rest of the night, and very often ever since." The old man returned to his seat, picked up his coffee, and took a sip from the coffee cup.

Michael had been watching intently with his hands clenched together, elbows on his knees, and his head resting on his hands. It was awkward for a moment, and then he sat upright, and then leaned back in his seat with his hands folded in his lap. "There really wasn't much you could have done different, it sounds like to me," Michael said, trying to justify what the old man had done. "I mean, she was the person pushing it, right?"

The old man looked at Michael with a deep, fatherly semi-smile, and his head bobbed slightly. Setting his cup down, he leaned forward and picked up the flyers and tickets. "Yeah, that's what I tried to tell myself at first. Then I remembered an old story about a guy that was with another man's wife and she started to get real friendly with him. He pretty much had to fight her off to run away from her, and she grabbed his clothes to keep him there. Long and short of it the guy's clothes tear off him and he runs away naked. THAT is a guy who really had no fault in what was happening and was REALLY committed to getting away from the situation!"

"Yeah, but I'm thinking running away naked on a cruise ship would get you the wrong kind of attention, especially from your wife," Michael chuckled as he answered.

"Pretty much," the old man replied with a grin, then returned to a bit more serious tone. "All kidding aside, Michael, this gets back to your original questions. We were talking about what is important to us, and why I hurried home, right?" Michael nodded, and the old man continued. "What is important to us we will give greater attention to in our lives. The greater the importance, the greater the attention. We are drawn to them, we protect them, and we cherish them. The thing is, we may say certain things are important, but what is really important gets our attention. Loyalty can be one of those things.

We can say we are loyal to our wife, our kids, our friends, but our lives will show what we are really drawn to, what's really important, and what's really in our heart. It always comes out, good, bad, or ugly. It always comes out. The guy in the story I just told you about? Now that guy was LOY-YAL - to the max. He's the sort of guy you want watching your back in a fight or a business deal, dating your daughter, or watching out for your family."

"So, I think I get it a little," Michael said in a way to try to pull the pieces together while looking into his coffee cup. "This loyalty thing is important to you. I understand that one for sure. My wife and I really hold our loyalty to each other as most important. And my partner Jimmy is as loyal as that guy in your story. He saved my life when I was in high school, literally, so I made him my right-hand man when I started my company. But what has that got to do with hurrying home?"

"Let me quickly answer that in two parts." There was the sound of what seemed like a distant siren getting closer. "I guess the city is finally waking up," the old man said, lifting his head in an upward nod to acknowledge the siren.

Michael nodded in agreement, then shook his head from side to side and in a sign of disenchantment with the moral decay in society evidenced by the siren. "Yeah, I have to be going pretty quick," Michael said, acknowledging the need for the shortened version of the story.

"First the loyalty and hurrying home question, then a quick end to my story," the old man replied. "Loyalty is one of those things that is a little hard to pin down. Our families, our friends, our jobs – each of these is an opportunity to experience a bond that, though unseen, cannot be broken. Like a mighty wind in the top of the trees, or that still small breeze just powerful enough to move one feather, loyalty lies waiting for us in our decisions. We really choose in an instant what will become the evidence of loyalty, or not. And we can make really good or really bad choices in the blink of an eye. But if we hold it dear to us, if we look and listen, we will see or hear the wind of loyalty's choice blow our way. We just have to choose it. That's why I chose to come home. I found myself beginning to judge you for just walking by – my 'They're all the same' comment, remember?

Michael nodded, a little puzzled. And the siren seemed to be getting closer. He began to wonder if there was something going on in this neighborhood that he did not even remember existed this close to downtown.

The old man continued, "I discovered after all of these things happened to me that it was my judging others that got me in the most trouble. When I judge others, I take my eyes off of what's important. I also found when that happens, if I stop and take a moment to consider the items in this chest, that helps to get me back on the right track." The old man reached into the chest and retrieved what looked like well-worn note cards, neatly rubber banded together in the middle. "Over these last few years when I hear what sounds like an important saying or famous quote about this subject, I write it down," he said as he waived the cards back and forth. "When I look at this stuff or read these cards, I remember what's important – things like loyalty. Once I finally figured that out, I promised myself that no matter where I was, if I found myself starting to slip into judging others or in any way slipping away from the important things in life, I would get to this chest and go through enough of the important things for me to get myself back on track. And it is important enough to hurry for, that's for sure."

Michael raised his eyebrows and nodded his head looking at the box, by way of giving the old man credit for his actions. "Hey, that's pretty cool. I can definitely respect your trying to stay the course. And I definitely respect your commitment to your way of doing that. Pretty cool." The sirens seemed to be getting louder, and Michael was convinced that they were headed for that neighborhood. It was in that moment that it hit him. This guy seemed really familiar – had he been on "America's Most Wanted" or something and was a criminal? He was a little strange – were the sirens for this old man? "Okay, well I really thank you for taking so much of your time with me, but I really need to be getting along."

"Wait," said the old man. "Let me just tell you this last part, about how I lost everything." The old man reached into the chest. He pulled out another paper-clipped sample of his life. This time it was two envelopes. One was a small one, like what gets clipped on flowers at the florist, and the other was a standard business class envelope with a window, which revealed something pink inside. "Like I said, my wife and I were pretty tore up about my mom. We got back late on a Friday and got the news from my brother and his wife. They met us at the dock and told us the story, as best they knew it. The company had a small private plane and they had flown in on it to meet us. It was a quick but seemingly endless flight back home. It was later still that night when we arrived and picked up the kids at my brothers. My wife and the kids and I spent most of the weekend crying and holding on to each other. Then, early in the evening on Sunday, there was someone at the door. It was a delivery guy from the florist. I answered and thought it was something for the family. Turns out it was for my wife from my partner!" the old man said in what was the closest thing Michael had heard to anger from the old man's voice. The old man held up the small envelope and quoted the words from the card. "'Sorry for your loss. If there is anything I can do, or you just need to talk, I am here for you'" and then just signed his initials. I recognized his writing. We had just gotten over one of our smaller arguments when she read the card out loud. I asked her why he was sending her flowers. She said it was because he was just trying to be nice. I said too nice. And so on. Pretty ugly."

"Wow. What did you do?" Michael asked, a little taken aback by the actions of the old man's partner.

"I was furious. We shouted at each other and I stormed out and went for a drive. I remembered I had Carla's number as I was driving, so I called her. Donny was on a trip, so we talked for an hour while I was just driving around. She suggested I come over, but I said I had to get back home and get some sleep. I was determined to get to work early and have it out with my partner, but I told her I would call her sometime."

"The next morning my wife and I barely acknowledged each other. I was actually just barely on time. I went storming into my partner's office to ask him what was going on, why he had sent that note to my wife. He was pretty condescending, and I reminded him that I was the owner and was not going to put up with this from him. And that's when he told me some more 'good news'." (The old man used the two fingers on each hand as he held them up and twitched them twice, as if he was putting quotes around those words in the air to accentuate their lack of sincerity.) "It seems that in our agreement that there was a clause that allowed each of us to exercise certain rights of ownership of the company, first me, then him. My rights of first refusal ended on the day I left for vacation. The next day, while I was on my wonderful 'vacation' (the double fingers again) that did me oh so much good, he exercised his rights to buy the company away from me. And he did it with my own money. He had even hired a new guy into the company to take his spot. Some wet behind the ears just out of college kid – William Walker was his name. I still remember him and his name. When he finished that little jewel of information, he handed me this envelope," he said picking up the pink windowed business envelope and waiving it slightly. "This is the pink slip he gave me that day when he let me go. He even had the nerve to have security escort me out without my things. Said he would have them packed in a box and sent to me by my successor – him!" The old man dropped the envelope back onto the coffee table.

"Then the rest just got really worse. I went home and told my wife what had happened, that I had lost my job. She yelled. I yelled. The kids heard us and began to cry. That started me looking for a job, any kind of job because my partner had black-balled me. I began drinking a little, then a lot. I kept being angry every day. More yelling. More crying. I even tried to call Carla. But when I explained what had happened, it seemed she was not too interested in a drunk without a job. My wife and I ended up in divorce court, and within a year she was married to my partner," the old man finished and sat back in his seat, and Michael sat back in his seat, a little puzzled. The sirens were clearly louder and closer now. And the old man's story began to seem too familiar, weirdly familiar.

"What exactly was the name of that agreement your partner executed?" Michael asked in a pale tone.

"Michael, Michael, Michael," the old man said, looking down a little and shaking his head. Then he looked up with those piercing eyes, "Of everything about the story I told you, that was what was most important to you?" asked the old man in an equally piercing vocal tone.

"Well, yeah," Michael replied a little surprised and puzzled by the question.

"Okay. Okay. We can do it this way," the old man commented strangely. "I believe the technical term is it is a form of a right of redemption."

Now Michael was beginning to get a little freaked out. "This old man must be a stalker. He must be the guy from that TV show," Michael thought to himself. And the sirens appeared to be almost outside the door. What should he do? He needed to get out of there, and fast. But too fast and the old guy might stab him, or shoot him, or who knows what. He decided to make his move and stood up abruptly to excuse himself.

"Hey, thanks for the coffee and cookies and great conversation, but I gotta be running along now," Michael said extending his hand for a fake handshake.

The old man stood up too, never removing his piecing stare from Michael now, even for a minute. "Like I said, my stories sometimes bother people. People don't want to think about what is really important to them always because then they have to realize it's all about choices, choices they make every day. We are all always loyal to what matters most to us, really matters. And the winds of loyalty, when they blow, they give us those chances to decide, to choose at that moment, what is important. The time we spend here is really just a string of choices. And like you said, times can change." The old man stuck out his hand to shake Michael's.

"Goodbye, errr... , what did you say your name was?" Michael asked, a little embarrassed that he had not asked earlier.

The old man grasped his hand and Michael felt something strange in his grip.

"It's Michael. Michael Stoneman," the old man replied in the velvet tone, with a wry smile at the corners of his lips as he shook the younger man's hand.

Michael grew pale and felt a little clammy. "But that's..., that's my name..." he said to the old man in a sort of fading voice. He was sure he was likely about to die. The sirens were outside. "This is it," he thought to himself.

The old man grabbed both their hands with his other hand and continued to shake them double handed. "It's time someone helped you wake up and smell the coffee kid," the old man said in a thick voice. "You're right this time Michael. It is your name," the old man continued in his velvety voice. "It's your name." This time there was a strange echoing in the old man's voice. The room started to dim, and he felt a little woozy like he was passing out or something. Had the old man really drugged him!?

"Michael!" came a shout from outside the door. Was that Marie? "Michael!" It was Marie! The police must have brought her with them. Thank God somebody must have seen them leave from downtown together! There was hope!

But nothing could have prepared Michael for what was to happen next, as his body began to shake involuntarily. Was it the old man's coffee?

CHAPTER 8:

SIRENS OF THE MORNING

"Michael!" Marie shouted, shaking his shoulders. He sat bolt upright with a start, completely wide eyed. He was sitting in his bed. Startled by his sudden movement, Marie jumped back a step from his bedside.

"What's wrong, honey? You okay? I was trying to wake you and you mumbled something about it being your name," Marie said, now taking a step toward him and putting her hand lovingly on his shoulder to comfort him. "And can you turn off that alarm please before it sounds off again? That crazy police alarm of yours is enough to wake the dead!" Marie walked away toward the end of the bedroom and continued packing their suitcases.

Michael blinked a couple of wide-eyed blinks to make certain he was really awake, then closed his eyes to yawn. He rubbed the top of his head then his forehead, down his face to the scruff of beard on his chin, then his neck. Leaning back slightly he reached back with his other hand and slapped the crap out of his police car alarm clock a couple of times until he finally hit the "Alarm Off" button – the light and siren on the top middle of the car. Jimmy had given him that alarm as a gag in college because he could never wake up in the mornings. Michael was always a deep sleeper and dreamer, even then. He slowly swung his legs off the bed, sitting on the edge, with his feet on the ground. Again, he rubbed his head as if to erase his dream.

"Well, that was interesting," Michael said, placing his hands on the edge of the bed, blinking wide-eyed and holding that look for a moment to clear his thoughts.

"What's interesting," replied Marie, not looking up, but continuing to look intently at her feet to accomplish packing for their trip.

"Oh, just a really, REALLY, crazy dream," he said, smiling. He snickered, "I guess I *really need* this vacation." He snickered because he had always believed that the best solution to almost any problem was more hard work. "It just seemed so real." He shook his head. "A bit strange, that's all," he finished as he stood to stretch. "What exactly are you making over there," Michael inquired as he looked at what could pass for a clothing sale at Macy's being stuffed into at least four suitcases that he could see.

"I am making sure we have everything for our trip, thank you for asking!" Marie's reply had that little edginess in it that usually happened when Michael tried to explain logic as it relates to their lives.

"Okayyy," Michael drug out his response. "But I am a little confused at all this."

"Honey, that is why you have me," she beamed. "First, I took out all of our shorts and tee's, and sorted them by color. For each outfit of yours, I have one that has complimentary colors. Hopefully ten outfits like that each will be enough. Then there are five casual slacks and polo shirts for you with sun dresses for me. I made sure to put in the one I wore on the Fourth to your company picnic. I remember how much everyone complimented me on it, especially Marge. Did you know she and Harry were thinking of taking a cruise? But Harry couldn't get away because his company got the job for the new stadium. That new stadium will be gorgeous! Can't wait till it's done!"

Michael, with arms crossed, began rubbing his chin in frustration. "She is on that roll again," he thought to himself. For some reason the older he got the more the credit roll – all those meaningless words at the end of a movie – got to him when she started on one. "Honey?" he asked out loud, trying to get her back to his question. "The Webster's dictionary people called. They said they would like to get some of their words back," he said with his sarcastic grin.

"Okay, okay! You don't have to get smart with me just because I want to say something!" replied Marie being jolted back to her explanation. "Okay, where was I? Oh yeah, right, the packing. Then I packed two swimsuits each. And I just found one yesterday at the mall that matches that orange pair that you have. Well, maybe not an exact match, but it does look good with it. And I was lucky because here at the end of the season it is hard to find a decent women's swimsuit, especially one that fits me." Marie was barely 5'5" tall, and feisty. But she was always so self-conscious about really nothing in Michael's eyes. He could never understand why she thought she was overweight. "I don't want to be on that ship with all of those pencils and me look like I just stepped out of a K-Mart ad for Plus sizes!"

"Honey, you are fine..." Michael began to say something he thought was encouraging, but the retort came faster.

"I don't need you to talk about my weight!" she snapped back now visibly slamming clothes into the next bag.

"I wasn't going to talk about your weight. I was..." Again, he was cut off.

"I got it! I got it! You were just going to say if it was important to me, maybe I should do something about it. I don't need you to fix it! I don't need you to fix me!" was Marie's full force blast as she began now to raise her voice.

"Fine. Fine," Michael spoke softly, raising his open palms to her in an attempt to calm the situation. "I just think you make too much of something that doesn't even exist. Let's just get back to the packing. You do know that we are only going for a week, right?" She nodded. "And they charge by bag for every bag we take." Always the money with Michael, always how much would something cost.

"Michael Stoneman, this is our first vacation in over five years. I can't believe you are going to give me one of your 'let's do this cheap' speeches?!" Her voice waivered a bit, and Michael thought she might begin to cry.

"Marie, I love you honey. You pack whatever you want. I just want us to get on this vacation and have a really good time." He strode over to her and gave her a hug, hoping to calm her for the moment.

"Well, I hope you mean that after all these years, really wanting to go on vacation and all," came the quick reply from Marie. She stopped her folding and contorting of the clothes for a moment. Looking up at him, she started in with "When you told me how Jimmy had arranged for us to get that special discount on the secluded voyage, I only said okay because you sounded like you were going to leave the office at the office. We had talked about a family vacation, but I only said okay because I wanted you to finally let go of work. And I know mom will love to have time with the kids."

"I know honey, I know," Michael replied. "It was just a really good deal. And when a friend helps you out like that..." He paused for a moment to listen to his words as he noticed a tiny white downy feather floating quietly along from the bed toward the suitcases. It must have come from one of the down pillows and was now being blown toward the suitcases, riding on the slightest of breezes coming from the air vents near the bed. Something about his words, and even the feather, got his attention, caused him to pause a moment, but then he continued, "Well, it would be bad manners to say no."

"That's fine. But if you don't hurry, you will be late for work," she said.

"Yes, dear," he replied, knowing it bugged her.

"And you will make me late dropping off the kids," she replied slightly irritated.

"Yes, dear," he said again smiling. She hated that dismissive response, but there was a certain impish side of him that just had to do it to get her goat, just a little.

"Don't be so smug!" she said, throwing a rolled-up pair of pants at him from the suitcase. He dodged the pants-to-the-head shot at the last minute, catching them in one hand. "The kids are all packed. They haven't stopped talking about going to your brothers to play with their cousins for a couple days. And I am not going to have you spoiling their vacation by being Mr. Slow Pants getting ready for work. Why do you have to go in anyway? You are the boss, right? You should have taken this day off to help me. But no, you had to go to work. I am going down to fix breakfast. The kids are hungry, and you still have to eat, too."

CHAPTER 9: BREAKFAST

"Come on, Mel. Sit up here at the table for me," Marie said reaching out her hands toward her youngest, her daughter Melinda, age five. Mel was busy this morning, playing with Johnny, age eight. They were pretend flying a plane through the dining room to get the pretend occupants to the cruise ship just off shore on the threshold to the kitchen. Not a threshold really, just an accented set-off that created a sense of separation in this great room. She had been trying to get their attention for what seemed like an eternity, but was really only just a few minutes. Their activity this morning was different, but the routine the same. Every morning she went through the chase and capture to get them to breakfast. The chasing and forced breakfast were just another of the tasks that Marie had reluctantly resolved herself to accept as a part of being mom. But today she was smiling, and practically dancing after the kids. Today she did not mind the routine, because today she would eventually leave on vacation.

Ba-ta-da-ta-da-ta-da! "Come and sit down for breakfast, Mel. You too Johnny! You guys want to go play with your cousins, right?" Marie was using her best mommy coaxing voice. Ba-ta-da-ta-da-ta-da! She grabbed the phone as she helped Mel into her child seat. Johnny took the seat to Mel's left, across from the kitchen. Recognizing Michael's mother's number on the Caller ID, she smiled a wide grin and she answered the phone with a bright, "Hello, Mom! How are you this wonderful morning?"

"Nana!!" came the eager squeal from Mel and Johnny simultaneously. The kids loved their Nana, and always wanted to talk when she was on the phone. "We want to talk to Nana! We want to talk to Nana!" came their cute little chant as they clapped their hands.

"Mel! Johnny! What have I told you about being polite when Mommy is on the phone? You can talk to Nana in a minute when Mommy is done," Marie lovingly scolded them. She set their plates in front of them with toast and jelly. She had the cordless held against her shoulder as she took the just finished lush yellow scrambled eggs in the skillet from the stove. "So, Mom, you are calling early. I was just about to call you. What's going on over there?" Marie continued to walk to the table and scooped out the steaming yellow eggs onto each of the kids' plates. "Come on guys, eat up."

There was talking at the other end of the phone. "Yes," was Marie's response. "Uh huh, I remember him. Haven't really seen him in a while." Pause. "Really? This early in the morning? I thought that he...," Marie had always been taught to respect her elders. "I thought Robert was more of a night person, you know." Pause. "Well, good for him. I'm glad to hear he is better." Pause. "Oh, okay, well I was hoping to ask a big favor of you, but that might get in the way of your plans." Pause. "Well, okay, I need to ask a favor. Your son is being Mr. Slow Pants this morning and overslept. He has not even come down for breakfast yet, so I know we are running late. I was hoping to drop the kids at your house on the way to work. I was supposed to run them by John's to play with the kids for a couple days, but I will be late if I do that now. Could you watch them today and let John pick them up after he gets off work, or maybe in the morning?" Marie asked, already knowing that Nana couldn't say no to Mel and Johnny. "Oh, that's so great! Yes, I know. I have no idea why he is running late to breakfast – he never runs late. Yes, I will tell him. Mom, the kids want to say hi. Okay, here they are." She handed the phone to an eagerly awaiting Mel, and then walked the skillet back to the stove.

"Hi Nana! Mommy says we get to come to your house today!" There was some muffled talking that could be heard. "What surprise? You going to make your special breakfast?

Okay, I love it! Yes, Johnny's right next to me. Okay, just a minute." Mel was responding to directions from Nana to lean over next to Johnny and hold the phone so they could both hear the surprise at the same time. "She wants to tell us a surprise where both can hear," Mel said to Johnny, leaning toward him with the phone tilted so he could get his ear near the receiver, too.

"Hi Nana!" responded Johnny, excitedly sharing the job of holding the phone with his sister. "What is the surprise? Yes. Yes, we can keep a secret," Johnny said looking at Mel as they both nodded. Suddenly their faces lit up with a glow. "Really?!" they shrieked together. "What's his name? We do? No, we won't tell. Love you Nana!" said Johnny, surrendering complete control of the phone to Mel.

"Love you Nana," said Mel. "Kiss, kiss." Mel was all smiles. "Here Mommy. Nana wants to talk to you," Mel said to her mother as she somewhat clumsily extended the phone back toward her mother returning from the kitchen. "Nana is getting a dog, but don't tell anyone. It's a secret!" Mel beamed.

"Mel!" said Johnny in disbelief, a little upset with his sister. "A secret means you don't tell it."

"I know that!" came Mel's squeaky indignant tone. "I just told Mommy not to tell!" Johnny just shook his head as he ate his food.

"Oh, really?" was Marie's reply, surprised at the news she just heard from Mel as she retrieved the phone just before it was about to drop out of Mel's hand. "Hi Mom. Yes, that was Mel. She tells me you're getting a dog? Mom, if you want something to be a secret probably telling a five-year-old is not your best bet. I know. No, I think it's great! Well, don't you worry about Mr. Slow Pants and what he thinks. Seriously Mom, I am sure Michael will be fine with it, or at least he will be when I get done with him!"

"Did I hear my name?" Michael had finally arrived at the bottom of the steps and was just coming into the great room by the dining table. Johnny looked at Mel, shaking his head holding a single finger to his lips for her to keep silent. She beamed a smile as she nodded and kept eating her eggs.

"And speaking of him, he just got here for breakfast. Okay, I have to run Mom. Yes, I will see you soon, and thank you. Yes, I love you too. Yes, he loves you too. Uh-huh. Okay. Bye," was Marie's response quickly to end the phone conversation. Setting the phone back in the cradle, she looked at Michael. "That was your mother. I wanted to have her watch the kids today because someone is making us late and I don't have time to run them by John's house." There was a scraping sound at the kitchen window. Startled, Marie and Michael looked up to see that a wind gust had just pushed the over-sized oriental maple up against the window. "Windy day."

"Okay, but I thought I heard the phone ring," was Michael's reply, retrieving his first cup of designer coffee from the counter near the window. "I am going to have to trim that tree when we get back."

"Oh, right. She called to tell me she had what was apparently another call from Robert this morning wanting to get together to talk. Scrambled?" inquired Marie, although Michael always had his eggs over easy. It was pay back for all the "Yes, dear" remarks earlier.

"Robert? Robert the lush? What did he do, drink all night? I don't think that would be a great idea," came Michael's judgmental commentary.

"Well, no, he got up early. Apparently, he has been sober for about a month now. Anyway, she won't be able to see him. I asked her to watch the kids today and she said yes. I guess she will have to put it off until tomorrow or the next day." The tree hit the window with another wind gust. "Scrambled?" she smiled looking at Michael.

Michael had a funny look on his face, like he was puzzled. Thoughtful, he replied, "No, I think I will skip breakfast this morning." Marie stopped in her tracks, eggs in one hand and skillet in the other. The kids stopped eating, looked at each other, and then at the dad. Michael never skipped breakfast. In fact, he always lectured about how important it was.

"Me too!" said Johnny, pushing away a plate with little on it.

"Me too! I'm skipping breakfast too!" said Mel, pushing away a half-filled plate. She was the slow eater.

"Fine, me too!" came Marie's half-puzzled, half-dismayed response. "I was just kidding about the eggs being scrambled." Putting the uncooked eggs back in the refrigerator, she placed the skillet and the kids' plates in the dishwasher. "And your mother is getting a dog for the kids and keeping it at her house."

"No, it's not about the scrambled thing. I just have a lot to get done, and this morning just seems a little strange. I just want to get to work and get back. And what's this about a dog? My mom doesn't need that kind of extra responsibility. She is getting to the place where she should be getting less responsibility in her life, not more. She needs to enjoy her retirement." It was the "Michael knows best" speech, and it was not well favored by Marie. Michael finished his coffee and placed his cup in the dishwasher.

Marie had her notebook computer open on the kitchen counter, looking at the vacation information in her email. Michael looked over her shoulder, something that always annoyed her. "Are you finished? Can I go to the next page yet?" Marie asked in a tone familiar to him as a "stop it" signal. "And you need to leave mom alone about the dog thing. She is a grown woman and you need to let her do what she wants. She just wants to have some fun with the kids. Let it go!"

"Yes, I am done," he said stepping to the sink to retrieve the dishwashing soap for the machine. "And I will let it alone, but I think I am right about the dog. What does it mean, secluded voyage?" The words were out of his mouth before he could stop them. Too late. Now Marie would know he bought the trip on price alone and knew very little about what the trip was about.

Marie shook her head as she clicked through her email quickly. "So, you didn't read about it BEFORE you bought it? I guess I should be thanking Jimmy for this trip since he got you to buy it sight unseen! It means we will be away from civilization. We will be on our own for much of the trip. We will get to enjoy each other's company. S-e-c-l-u-d-e-d? Get it?"

There was something troubling about the thought of being THAT secluded, but Michael could not quite put his finger on it. "So, do

you think they have cell phone reception?"
This was not a good day for Michael and his
topic selection for their communications.

"I can't believe you want to keep your cell
phone on for our first vacation in five years!
No, there is no reception!" Marie was clearly
upset as her voice waivered, and the corners
of her eyes became a little misty. This time
the tree hit the glass even harder, and they
both jumped.

"No, honey, it's not that. It's just... I don't
know. I'm sure it will be fine," Michael tried
to encourage her as he put his arm around her
shoulder. "I need to get going. I am going to
call our yard guy to have him do something
about that tree. It would be a shame to come
home to find out a tree broke into our house
while we were gone!" he chuckled. He
grabbed his jacket and computer bag and
headed towards the door. He heard Marie
close her computer. But what she said next
stopped him dead in his tracks as he opened

the door and turned to wave goodbye to the kids.

"Maybe we'll meet some nice people on the trip, and make some new friends," came Marie's voice, with a sort of velvet quality to it. The tree hit the window, but Michael didn't move. "What's wrong?" Marie asked, seeing Michael's face going a little pale.

Slowly, Michael shook his head. "Nothing. It's all good. Have to go," was Michael's somewhat clumsy reply as he headed out the door.

CHAPTER 10:

AN ALTERNATE ROUTE

ichael pulled out of the garage and sped off in his 325i. He was actually ahead of schedule, but his mind was not on his schedule, even a little. All he could think of were Marie's words, "Maybe we'll meet some nice people on the trip, and make some new friends." It was a little foggy, but he was sure that was what the old man had said in his dream. The thoughts of his crazy dream had been filling with the mist that infiltrates the memories of them as the reality of the day progresses. But all of that mist was cleared up in an instant like some mega defroster on the windshield of life with her words. How did she know? He looked at his dash clock. There was time to be shaved off of today's schedule, if he could pull it off. He would have to contact the office. Then it came to him – he must have been talking in his sleep. Of course! That was it. She had heard him and just repeated the words, not even knowing that he had said them in his sleep. Absolutely! That was it. "Huhhhh," he let out a sigh of relief. "Come on Michael, come on. Just a few hours and you will be on vacation. Don't get loopy on me now," came the Michael morning talk-to-me self-pep talk. His phone read "7:40 AM" with four bars. As he hit the speed dial for work, there was a gust of wind that shoved him slightly to the shoulder. "Four bars. Well, that's different from the dream," Michael said to himself remembering that in the dream he had no signal. He was dialing his assistant's direct line. "Lilly, I hope you are in."

"Good morning, Mr. Stoneman. Interesting weather today, don't you think," came the most professional voice of his assistant, Lilly James.

"Why yes Lilly, it is, I guess. And how many times do I have to tell you, it's Michael? Mr. Stoneman was my father."

"Yes, I know Michael, and a good man he was, too. I enjoyed working for him for many years. Sometimes I just like to hear the sound of the name one more time. But I will do as you wish, Michael. I assume you are on your way in; how can I be of service?" Lilly had worked for his father at his insurance agency. After his father died, several people tried to help keep the agency moving forward. His mother still had her credentials, so she went back to work in the office like the old days. Even old man Silverman came back once or twice to help out, although he tried not to let anyone know. When Michael got out of college, he tried to keep the agency going, but his specialty was computers. When he began writing programs for the insurance and investment industry, it became clear that was his calling. The side jobs became the primary revenue, and ultimately took off after a few years. After discussing it with his mother, they sold the book of business to Silverman's nephew.

"Well, I was thinking that perhaps I could save myself some time and swing by Silverman's to hammer out the final details and get the contract signed. It would save me a trip later. I thought perhaps you could make that call for me to try to get him to see me early." Michael was trying to get Lilly to use her social capital with Silverman. After all, she had been his administrative assistant as well when Silverman and his dad had the agency together. When Silverman wanted to go after only the wealthiest of businesses and people, his dad said he just could not walk away from the little guy. His dad bought Silverman out and they both went on to do well in their own markets. Or at least his dad did until he died.

"That won't be necessary," was Lilly's simple reply.

"Oh?" Michael's voice revealed his puzzled thoughts. "And why would that be?

"Because he already called me about a half hour ago. Silverman said to tell you if you called on the way in to say come on over. The agreement was fine as submitted, and he would sign it with you when you arrived."

Michael slowed his car slightly without realizing it. "Wait, you are saying Manny Silverman doesn't want to argue over ANYTHING in the contract? Are we talking about the same guy?" Michael's astonishment was showing. He got back up to speed and changed lanes to make the turn toward Silverman's offices.

"Michael, Emanuel Silverman is a good man. I know you and everyone think he is harsh, but he has a good heart. He and your father were very good friends before..." She could not bring herself to say the words.

"Before my dad died?" was Michael's reply. "Yes, I know all about that. But you have to admit, this is not like him. I mean, when was the last time you ever heard of him doing this? Is he in a hurry or something, is it a trick, what? Have you heard anything from any of your sources?"

"By my sources I assume you mean Barbara," was Lilly's somewhat cooled response. Barbara had left Michael's dad's company with Silverman. Manny had offered her Lilly's job at his new company, and she jumped at the chance. Lilly and Barbara grew up together and had remained best friends through it all. "Barbara said Manny has been acting different for about a month now. Taken on a wide variety of social "projects", if you will. Called up some of the people he has fired over the years and hired them back to work on a special project. Even helped Robert with his problems and mended their fences. She said Manny had confided something odd to her at the beginning of it. Something about a dream he had."

Michael slammed on the brakes to avoid running a red light, and the winds blew hard. "Did you say a dream?" Michael asked struggling to keep his voice from wavering.

"I know, I know. But why look a gift horse in the mouth? Anyway, he is expecting you. And he is in a hurry. He is going to leave after meeting with you to take his wife on vacation." Lilly, hearing the impact on Michael, tried to smooth over her remarks.

"Well, alrighty then." It was Michael's canned response he used when something caught him off guard. "Look, I am almost there. I have just a couple things to wrap up at the office."

"Michael, I already told everyone that you were going to take today off to help your wife pack and get on the road early. Once Manny and you sign, why not just send it with a courier? Mr. Jimmy seemed more than happy to have the show to himself a day early." Lilly was never a Jimmy fan.

Michael chuckled. Lilly was always looking out for him, as she had done for his father. "Let me guess," came his voice with the sparkle of the chuckle still in it. "You and Marie have been plotting against me again." Ignoring the Jimmy comment, Michael was smiling, and it showed in his voice.

"Well, of course Michael. We women have to stick together!" was Lilly's quick-witted reply.

"Okay, then that is what I will likely do. But there will be another courier coming in from the bank to see me with an envelope. Would you sign for it and lock it in your desk until I get back?" Michael was still the detail man.

"Certainly, Michael. You and Marie have a great trip, and don't worry about anything here. I will make sure all goes well." And Lilly meant it. Michael knew he could trust her. She was as loyal to Michael as she was to his father before him.

Michael pulled into the parking garage at Silverman's. "Well, I need to run Lilly. I am here at Manny's. Let's hope his new-found outlook on life lasts at least until we finish this deal. Wish me luck."

"I will. And I will throw in a prayer for good measure." Lilly's voice was steadfast, and serious. Michael knew she was a religious person.

"Thank you," was his quick reply as he hung up. As he got out of his car and headed into the building, he was muttering to himself. "What are you up to Manny Silverman?" he said to himself, quietly. He couldn't wait to see how this would all play out as he stepped into the lobby.

Barbara was standing next to the receptionist's desk, giving her pointers on the phone system. "Good morning Mr. Stoneman. Mr. Silverman has been expecting you. Right this way please," she said as she began walking toward the president's office.

That was Barbara. Like Lilly, the consummate professional assistant. Perhaps she could provide Michael with some insight. About halfway to the office, Michael stepped next to her side and asked, "So, Barbara, how is business here these days?" It was a weak attempt at small talk, and an obvious attempt at gaining more information.

She turned her head and slowed slightly. "Business is very good for us," Barbara responded smiling like a child with a secret they know you want to hear. "What makes you ask?"

Michael stopped, forcing Barbara to stop to turn to him. "Well, it is a little different for me to have an appointment with Manny like this. Everything okay with him?"

Now Barbara was beaming. "Well, I believe it is. But perhaps when you speak with him you might ask?" She turned and continued the twenty paces or so to the president's office and tapped on the door. "Come in!" was the response from within. She opened the door and gestured to Michael to enter. "Mr. Silverman, Mr. Stoneman is here for his appointment." With appropriate etiquette, she stepped out of the office closing the door behind her.

Emanuel Silverman was a slender, sixty-something exceptionally talented insurance agency and investment house owner. A full head of once jet black and only now graying hair sat above his prominent facial features – strong jaw, robust nose, piercing brown eyes, and that smile that he only saved for special occasions. He was smiling now. "Michael, it is so good to see you! How are the wife and children, and that wonderful lady, your mother?" Manny closed his white board presentation cabinet where he had been making notes with a marker and strode with arm outstretched to shake Michael's hand. It took Michael by surprise and he stopped not far from the door.

Silverman, unphased at Michael's sudden pause, strode the entire distance to Michael. Shaking his hand like he had just been rejoined to a long-lost war buddy, he motioned to one of the two chairs in front of Manny's desk. "Michael, please have a seat. So, tell me, the family?"

Michael was trying to get comfortable with what was happening. He never knew Manny to be anything but all business – no "shop talk". Yes, he still was wearing his three-piece pinstripe suit (Manny was old school), with a lightly starched white shirt and burgundy-over-black dotted power tie, and his entire appearance was immaculate, but the rest?! "There are two chairs away from the desk with a coffee table in front and Manny actually sits in one to speak with me? He wants to chat about my family, not as an elevator speech filler but like he really cares what the response is." Michael's head was spinning with thoughts. Yet somehow, there was something he liked about the new Manny. Maybe it was just not the "wrestling over nothing until the real issue emerges and you are too tired to fight anymore" contract negotiation style that had vanished. "They are good, they are good. And how is Elizabeth?" Elizabeth was Manny's wife.

"Ah," said Manny wistfully in a tone Michael had not heard from Manny in more years than he could remember. "Elizabeth, my princess, is as beautiful and wonderful as the day we met." Was Manny smiling as he gazed out the oversized Executive Office windows to the skyline? "But I think you are here for something," he said smiling still. Manny rose and took the two steps to his desk, pressed the intercom, and said, "Barbara, could you bring in those items we discussed? Thank you." He returned to his seat, and Barbara emerged through the door behind them.

"Here are the items you requested, Mr. Silverman." Barbara extended her hand, holding some folders that Michael recognized as the logoed binders the Silverman Group used when they signed completed contracts.

Manny was a stickler for presentation. But why more than two of the copies of the deal?

Manny took the folders, placed them on the coffee table immediately in front of he and Michael. The coffee table had a short stack of books on it (the one on top was titled *Tinman to Ironman* or something like that by... Swanson, maybe? There were a couple open packages of sticky notes on it covering up some of the letters. And there were two books that were well dog-eared and marked with sticky notes hanging out, that were opened to specific pages face down. Michael could read the titles, even upside down. One was *The Cash Flow Quadrant* by Robert Kiyosaki and the other *Launch a Leadership Revolution* by Woodward and Brady. "Looks like you have been doing some interesting reading," was Michael's comment, with a curiosity that was only matched by the expression on his face. There were several legal pads with copious notes, and even some 3x5 cards with the famous Silverman chicken scratch on them.

"Reading? Oh yes, reading..., definitely reading. And a whole lot more." Opening the first two folders to the "Sign Here" marked page, he signed and dated it. "Your turn," said Manny, sliding the documents in front of Michael and extending to him his Mont Blanc.

Michael was stunned but tried to hide his response. It made Manny chuckle lightly. As Michael took the pen and leaned forward, he could see that these were the documents he personally had prepared on his own company's letterhead. They were the originals, with no mark-ups for changes. "No changes required, Manny?" Michael asked, still trying to contain his surprise.

"Michael, you and I have been dealing with each other since... since the days with your father and me. In all that time I don't think I ever mentioned it." Manny paused slightly. "You write a good contract. You always try to be fair with me. And in the past, I have enjoyed making you work too hard for me to authorize them. Seems now like a waste of time, don't you think?"

Michael's mouth dropped open slightly. He could no longer hide his surprise. "Manny, is everything okay? I mean, really okay?" The words just came out before he could stop himself. He had known Manny since childhood. Over the years, however, Manny had become aloof and distant, focused on business only. It was business at the expense of all else. He had developed an excellence in "negotiations" which really meant he would wear out his opponents to get what he wanted. A few months ago, Michael's question would have drawn a scowl and a harsh lecture in business etiquette from Manny. But this was not a few months ago.

"Michael, when a man gets to be my age, it can be easy to be caught up in routine, in the matters of business, in things that just consume time." Manny stood and strode over to the oversized windows overlooking the skyline. One hand was suspended by a thumb in his vest, the other had retrieved a pocket watch which Manny was gazing at. "We can lose track of time. You know," Manny said, turning slightly toward Michael, "your father gave me this watch when we parted ways. Most men would have taken me to court, tried to black-ball me in the insurance business. But not your father. When I told him we needed to work with higher-end clients, all he could say was, 'What about the little guys? They need us too.'" Manny paused for a moment, gazing into the past, looking out the window. "What about the little guys?" he muttered, then briefly looked at his feet to gain his composure. "We finally went our separate ways – me to the high-end insurance and investment clientele, and your father to everyone else. There were a few of the high-end folks that stayed with him, which I did not understand then. And when I left, I took Barbara and Robert and others. Your father wished me luck. He gave me this watch and that Mont Blanc as parting gifts. Said if I was going to work with the wealthy, I needed to look the part." Manny paused with some emotion. "The inscription says, 'Loyalty is a timeless treasure. Thank you for sharing it with us.'" Michael noticed the flags in the flag memorial outside the building were suddenly standing straight out from the wind gust, and then relaxed. "When we started up here, we had only a few clients. Those were some challenging times."

"Yes, I remember my dad talking about it sometimes. I know that must have been difficult," came Michael's reply, also feeling the emotions of those days, but holding them in.

"Yes, I am sure you did. But there is something you didn't know. Your father was the one bankrolling us. It was rough on my pride, I can tell you that, but he insisted. We signed an agreement that Benjamin drew up. Your father had it set up so that in time, he could redeem stock in our company from the profits. The idea was that the earnings would pay for it all, and eventually you and your mother would have a little something to rely on later in life. I had all but forgotten about it until about a month ago."

Michael struggled with his emotions. This was news, good news he thought. But rethinking his dad's demise always made him uncomfortable. "What happened a month ago?"

"That is a good question, Michael, a very good question," Manny replied returning to his seat and opening up the remaining two folders. "I guess the best way to put it is I met up with someone that reminded me of what is important in life, and that loyalty is one of those precious things. And trust." Michael noticed the flags were now really dancing in the breeze outside in the bright sun, waving the red, white, and blue with a sharp snappiness. "You know, your father was a dreamer."

Michael snapped out of the emotions of the moment. Mostly when people said that about his dad, it was not a compliment. "I prefer to think of him as a visionary," Michael replied in a politically correct dry tone.

"That too," responded Manny. "Anyway, the result is good for you." Manny was signing some type of certificate in the folder, and then a document in each folder. "I spoke with your mother earlier in the week and she stopped in to sign off on these papers. She said she wanted you to have the stock. And she wanted you to have the earnings. Seems they have accumulated in the last couple years when times have been better. If you will just sign here below your mother's signature on both of these documents, this certificate is yours." Manny slid the folder over in front of Michael. "And so is this." Manny extended his hand and in it was a cashier's check, made out to Michael Stoneman, for $50,000. "Not a great deal of money, but not bad for a start. Now that you own the stock outright, you will be able to get a good return like this every year."

Michael was speechless. It was as if his father had reached out from the grave to give him a surprise gift. "Manny, I..." Michael's words were choppy. He composed himself and signed the papers. He realized that Manny could have held on to this forever, and he and his mother would have been none the wiser.

"Your mother said she thought this would be a great time for you to get this. Said you and your wife are going to take a vacation?" Manny inquired, watching as Michael authorized both copies of the document.

"Yes. Yes, we are. I have been trying to button up a few things today and we are supposed to get underway tonight. Thank you for this Manny. If you had never said anything, we would never have known," was the best Michael could come up with as he now placed both of his copies in the two folders and the check into his briefcase.

Manny raised his hand to waive off the compliment. "Vacation. There is a word I have not used often enough over the years. It is good that you are taking time away with Marie." Manny reached forward to the coffee table and took his copies and tapped the sides, acting as if he was straightening them to excess. He stopped while still holding the bottom edge to the coffee table. He looked at them, and then turned his gaze out the windows in the direction of the flag memorial. "It is hard to believe it took me over sixty years to find out what is important in life. Family. Friends. Loyal friends. Friends you can trust." The flags outside began to flutter and dance in the exuberant breeze once more. "You father was a friend, but he was more than that. He was loyal to those he cared about. I always felt, even after he was gone, that his heart was always here with me, encouraging me to keep going." Now even the trees across the street were swaying in rhythm with the flags. "This whole thing with the stock here. Like I said, it was your father that really helped to bankroll our business when we left." Manny had to pause. He looked down at the floor and pretended to adjust his reading glasses. "So," he said lifting his head and forcing himself to move the conversation forward, "I have decided to do something about it. I am restructuring the way we are organized here. And Elizabeth and I are going to take a vacation."

"That's great Manny. Europe? The Caribbean?" Michael asked with forced enthusiasm, deliberately looking past the reorganization comment. He was trying in his own way to help Manny get past the emotional moment.

Manny smiled another uncharacteristically huge smile. "No sir," he said as he half stood to reach for a portfolio on his desk. Sitting back down he laid it open on the coffee table in front of them. Michael was a little shocked. It was an owner's portfolio for an RV. And the picture on the cover of the brochure inside looked familiar somehow. "My dear Elizabeth and I are going to see the U.S. of A.! She has talked about this for a long while. I think your mother and she have talked about it many times. Anyway, I realized over the last month that this is something that she always wanted to do. For me, I just want to do something with her."

Michael truly was not ready for this revelation. "Where did you get the information, and the RV?" was all he could think to say.

"I bought it from my nephew. You remember Jacob, right? Well, he got a dealership and is in the RV business now, Silverman's RV World over there off of 55. He gave me a great deal." Manny was beaming over the brochures and information like a kid with a new toy.

"When do you leave, and how long will you be away? We will want to be working on your project, but we can put it off until you get back." Michael was back on business.

"We leave either tonight or tomorrow morning. And I am not certain when we will be back. It could be a while. But don't worry. You can still go ahead with the project. My new Executive Vice President will be minding the store while I am away." Manny had an impish grin on his face, like he was hiding something but dying to tell it. After a short pause, he could not hold it in. "I am promoting Barbara to Executive VP. She pretty much runs the place anyway. She knows all of the ins and outs here. She will be overseeing the project from our side. And I have brought back some people to work on a special project." If he had an impish grin before, this was full-fledged gnome. "They will be working with Barbara to redesign the organizational structure of our business I mentioned. In my reading (gesturing to the books on the coffee table) I have come to realize we were never set up to be the most successful we could be. Instead, I ran the sales guys through here like so many cattle. Guess I forgot much of what your father had taught me through the demonstration of example. But I am going to change all that. From now on, everyone that works here gets a shot at making their mark, at making as much or more than me, if they set it up right."

To say Michael was stunned would be the understatement of the decade. "Okay, Manny, since you brought it up, why do you want to change? You have done pretty good for yourself; I think everyone would agree. Of course, some people come and go. That's the nature of things. You gave them a job while they were here. You owe them nothing. And everyone has a chance to make more than you?!? Sounds like one of those pyramid pitch deals," Michael said with a bit of a snicker, his sad attempt at comfort.

Manny looked at Michael with a bit of a glare, and for just a moment, Manny was back. Then, a wry smile came to his face. Leaning forward in his chair toward Michael, he started in. "Okay Michael, let's have this discussion. What is your dream?"

"Excuse me?" came Michael's startled reply.

"Your dream," replied Manny in a pseudo question. Not allowing for a response, he quickly continued, "Let me guess. As a child it was your dream to sit in a cubicle or office all day, racking your brain over the exact computer programming code, and why it wasn't working. You hoped you would never have to have a vacation. You secretly wanted to spend 80 hours a week working away from your family, always living in the fear of getting sick or something happening to prevent you from working. Without you the business eventually would fold because YOU were the magic. And you wanted to eat all that fast food so your health could go downhill, working until you were too old to enjoy retirement, and drinking wine when you got home just so you could sleep. Oh yeah, and you dreamed of never really helping others." Manny was being ruthless in this pursuit, noticing Michael wincing slightly at his words. "And let me show you something," he said as he stood and moved to the white board cabinet, opening it and taking the marker in his hand.

Manny drew a circle at the top center of the whiteboard and wrote "Manny" next to it. "This is me." Just below that circle he drew three circles, labeling them CFO, COO, and VP-S&M. "These are my three top guys. Underneath of them he drew the seven circles that represented his managers from the various departments and two remote offices. "These are my managers." Under these he drew what looked like two rows of fifteen circles each, with the letters "etc." at the end of the second row. "And these are all the sales guys I have had over the years, even though we only have maybe 30 now, we have had literally hundreds go through here."

"And your point is?" inquired Michael, with just a slight hint of sarcasm.

"My point is simple," replied Manny as he drew the obvious three-sided figure around this group. "What does that look like to you?" he asked Michael, gesturing in his direction.

"Our corporate structure?" came Michael's response, again with the same tone.

"Hmm. I think the word you used a minute ago was pyramid. And in this pyramid, who makes the most money? I do. Who has a real opportunity to make as much or more than me? No one. How many lives could I have changed that I didn't, even Robert's? And for what? Those chicken scratches on that damn board? My name on the door? The right to come back and do it all over again day in and day out, never taking time to have a family, take a vacation, breathe the air? What if we would have kept all those people because they had a dream of doing something great, something better for their families, and they saw the chance of making that happen here? After all, either way, I spent the resources to train them. How big would we have become? And the sad truth is, I am sure based on some preliminary numbers that I would have made ten to a hundred times more than I make now trying to hold on to it all." Manny let his arms finally fall to his side, weary from talking with his hands. He smiled. "No more." He drew a couple large X's through the triangle. "No more. I don't know what they will come up with and don't care. I am sure it can and will be better than this." Closing the cabinet, he returned to his chair. "And as I said, Barbara is the Executive Vice President now and she will take great care of you on this contract."

"Okay." Michael paused. "I am sure that will be fine for us. We will look forward to moving forward with her on this." Michael looked at his Rolex. "I better get going. Still need to get some things done today and get back to my lovely wife as well. She wanted me to help her pack." Michael was trying to recover from the Barbara announcement, and the reorganization project. Sheesh! The Manny he used to know would never have promoted his administrative assistant to a VP position, much less give every sales guy a shot. Manny was definitely different now.

The two of them stood up. Manny shook Michael's hand with the same bravado as when he had entered the room. "You know, some time you should talk with Robert." Michael shook his head and looked down. "I know, I know, but he has changed," Manny asserted. "Everyone deserves a second chance." With that he gave Michael's hand one more solid shake, and the meeting ended.

CHAPTER 11:

A HERO REVEALED

"Well, that was interesting," Michael thought to himself as he gingerly walked to his car. The day was starting to get away from him, and there remained much to do. What was going on with Manny? First the agreement signed without an argument. Then the $50,000 stock redemption deal that neither he nor his mother knew existed. Then the reorganization bomb. Finally, Manny bought an RV to take his wife on a vacation? Were they really going to become snowbirds and head south every winter, let alone in this nicer weather? Michael smiled and chuckled to himself as he thought of Manny behind the wheel of an RV in a three piece suit. Whatever was going on, this was turning out to be a very different day than he had anticipated, and it was good. Now he needed to refocus.

Reaching his Beamer, Michael signaled and unlocked the doors. Throwing his case in the seat beside him, he revved the engine and sped away from the parking garage. He scrolled quickly through his messages and noticed that Marie had called around 7:40am. "Hmm," he muttered to himself, "Guess I was talking with Lilly." There was also a message from Lilly's number that had come in during the meeting with Manny. He wanted to find out what was up at home, but business first was his mantra. He pressed to hear the message from Lilly.

"Mr. Stoneman, I need to speak with you. Please call me when you get this." There was odd strain in Lilly's voice. The last time he had heard her like that was when her friend had been in a serious car accident. "Something very odd is going on here. If you do come in, call me first. It's important." The message was cryptic, but the emotion in

Lilly's voice was very real. Something was up, and it did not sound good. Michael was heading home but changed directions to head to the office. It might be nothing, but Lilly was a loyal employee and it sounded as if she really needed his help. He pressed call back.

Lilly answered, but in a soft voice, as if she did not want to be heard at her end. "Michael, I am so glad you called." Her voice sounded shaken, and she almost never called him Michael until he asked her to first.

"Lilly, are you okay? Your message sounded urgent, but I wasn't sure what you were trying to say." Michael was trying to be calming.

"Michael, there have been some people come and go from Jimmy's office. I think they are lawyers from Benjamin's office." Benjamin, Manny's brother, had been the family's personal and business attorney/firm since his father's days. "And then Jimmy took something into your office and stayed in there a while. When I went in to see if he needed something he was in your chair with his feet on the desk gazing out the window. The folder was on your desk. When I asked if there was something I could get for him he said no, that he was just trying it on for size. He had a funny grin on his face, and then he told me not to let anyone into the office until next week. When I asked why, he said he would explain it to me Monday, and that he and I would be working more closely in the future. What is going on Michael? Are you going to make me work for Jimmy?"

"No, Lilly, no, you will be working for me, always. I do not know what is going on, but I am headed that way now. I am sure everything will be fine." Michael was doing his best to be reassuring, but he was taken aback at the thought of Jimmy in his office. And trying his chair on for size? What was that?

"Okay, Michael. But I don't think anyone is expecting you. And Jimmy locked your office I think." Lilly was beginning to calm down.

"Oh, and I almost forgot. Your mother called. She said she was going to meet with Robert at that diner. I guess he has been calling to talk to her for a few days or something. She just wanted you to know where she was."

"I actually will pass by there on the way in, but I thought she was going to be taking care of the kids." It bothered Michael to think that his mother would take the kids to hang out around the town drunk. "I will see you soon."

Michael called their attorney's office. "This is Michael Stoneman. Is Benjamin available? I see. I need you to take a message to him for me. Please ask him to pull the organizational documentation for our company and review it. There are some items I want to be clear on about the stock redemption agreement. That's right. Tell him I will call back later. Thank you." He hung up.

Michael pressed the button for the message from Marie, frustrated by what he had just heard. "Hello there Mr. Slow Pants," came that loving and playful voice of Marie in her message. "When you did not eat breakfast, I was able to get the kids in the car quickly and dropped them at your brothers. I told them we would drop the luggage off this afternoon. You did remember you said you were getting off early to help me, right? And I called your mother to let her know that I would not be bringing the kids by, that I was headed in for a short day at work. She said something about how that worked out well. She was going to go ahead and meet up with Robert then at the diner. Guess he has been calling about wanting to talk to her. You know Mom. Probably going to have pie and coffee with him and just listen. Okay honey, come home early so we can get going. Love you! Bye." Marie always said I love you at the end of her messages. As he set his phone on the console, a strong gust of wind came up and pushed on the car. He let his phone go to grab the wheel with both hands, and his phone careened into the passenger side foot well.

"Steady," Michael said to himself, holding the car under control. Michael was relieved. At least his kids were not going to be around Robert. He turned the corner by the diner and slowed slightly. He wanted to look in the windows of the diner to see if his mother was sitting in her favorite booth. He had to keep his eyes on the road, but sure enough, there was his mother. And it looked like Robert, only not in rags. Had Robert actually cleaned up a bit? Michael sped up as he continued towards the office. He was a few blocks past the diner now. "My mother the caregiver having pie and coffee with the town drunk. I hope he doesn't upset her," Michael was talking to himself, on autopilot again. Suddenly, it hit him. He hit the brakes and pulled to the curb in some open parking and turned the car off. His mouth had dropped slightly open. "Could it be? That's... that's just crazy." Michael had suddenly remembered his dream, or parts of it. Another wind gust hit. "Marie said something about meeting people on vacation. Mom is getting a dog." What was it the old man said... time is not fixed? "Marie was not late, so she dropped the kids off at his brother's. Mom is having pie and coffee with the town drunk. The town drunk had something important to say. Dreams are supposed to be about the past or crazy imaginary futures. But this is like, like the dream is coming true." Could that really be? Several strong gusts rocked the car. "Okay, Michael, okay." Talking to himself, he was now trying to calm himself down. "You really need this vacation. There has to be a logical explanation. Just calm down." He thought for a moment. He was still close to the diner. Maybe Manny was right. Maybe he should talk with Robert and set him straight on a few things about his mother. Michael fired up his Beamer and, pulling quickly out of the parking into a vacant side street, he spun it around to head back to the diner. He was a man on a mission.

From down the street he could see Joe, the hot dog pushcart guy. Joe and the Diner owner Marty were good friends. Joe always stopped by before the lunch hour to stock up. They had a deal where Joe could get his supplies cheaper, and Marty would get extra boxes delivered and put in his walk-in cooler for Joe. Joe was stocking up now. As Michael drew closer, he saw several empty parking spaces across the street from the Diner. Pulling into park, he looked to see if his mother and Robert were still there. He saw his mother stand up very quickly and shake her head, getting something out of her purse. He turned away to make sure he didn't hit anything. Getting out of the car, he clicked the fob to lock it. He was now directly across from Joe but could not see his mom. Robert was still in his seat, looking down at the table. There was another gust of wind. As Michael began to cross the street, he looked in horror at what was unfolding. His mother was coming quickly down the few Diner steps, looking for something in her purse. She was just about to round Joe's cart, when out of the corner of his eye Michael caught a glimpse of the city bus accelerating through the intersection. His mother was headed right in front of it when she passed the cart. All of this was happening in seconds, but it was like it was slow motion for Michael, who was continuing across the street. No time to think. With two giant steps and a gust of wind at his back, he leaped forward, right past the front of the bus. He tackled his mom, grabbing hold of her and turning in one smooth motion so that he would be the one to hit the ground. He landed in Joe's stack of empty boxes, which helped to cushion the blow. The city bus driver slammed on the brakes and the bus came to a screeching halt right where Michael had just passed by in the air moments before.

"You okay, Emma? Michael?" It was Joe, reaching down to help them up.

"You okay Mom?" Michael asked, still breathing heavy from the adrenaline and the athletic moment.

"I am fine, I am fine." Emma, a silver haired slender woman now in her sixties, was straightening her simple blue dress and adjusting some of the mysteries in her purse. "Now I understand what your father meant when he said your high school football skills would come in handy one day." She managed to put a smile on her face. Emma always made the best of every situation.

"Emma?" came a voice from behind them. Michael turned to the voice, only to see the unexpected. Robert stood before him, neatly dressed in casual slacks and a shirt that made him look like he just stepped out of a Sears's ad. In his earlier times Michael would have smelled the Wild Turkey on Robert's breath at this distance. But there was not a trace. In fact, Robert's speech and his eyes were very clear. Robert actually looked good. "Michael, are you and your mother okay?" he asked.

Michael nodded toward him. "Robert. Yes, we are fine. Let's all go inside for a moment. I want to speak with you." Robert nodded and turned. Both he and Michael helped Emma back inside to her favorite booth.

Michael sat next to his mother, and Robert positioned himself across from them both. "Can you tell me what was so important that you had to tell my mother? So important and upsetting that you almost got her killed?!" Michael's voice was starting to have that edge to it just before it got real nasty.

"Michael! What just happened is not Robert's fault!" Emma said in a semi scolding tone. "I was just being careless."

"It's okay Emma. Michael is right to be concerned," Robert responded to Emma's scolding as he reached out to pat one of her hands on the table. "Michael, I am glad you are here. I thought you had left for vacation. But I wanted you to hear what I had to say as well." Robert was looking Michael straight in the eyes. No flinching, no looking away from the embarrassment of being the town drunk. Clearly, Robert was becoming a person with purpose in his life. He continued, and the subject was a sensitive one for Michael.

Michael, it is about your father. There is something I need to tell you. I need to set the record straight about that day..." Robert paused and looked down at his hot cup of coffee cradled by his two large hands. "John was always good to me. Heck, John was good to everyone. Even when Manny left and took some of us with him. John helped us get a start."

"And I love how you have honored him with what you did with that start!" snapped Michael. If Robert thought he was going to be getting sympathy from Michael, he was making one more in a long line of bad decisions. Emma slapped lightly at Michael's hand on the table as if to signal him to stop being abrasive.

"You are right again Michael. And you are right to be angry. I cannot change what has happened. I cannot undo the years of mistakes. But I can tell the truth about one." Robert took a sip of coffee. "I know what everyone says about the accident."

"Do we really have to do this? You almost cost my mother her life. Don't you get that?" Michael was leaning forward as he spoke, and he felt himself clench his fists.

"Michael, please just listen. It didn't happen the way everyone thinks." Robert took another sip. "Your dad was the hero, not Jimmy."

Michael was stunned by what he was hearing. For years the story had been told to him over and over the same way. His father had hit the rock in the stream. Jimmy pulled everyone to shore. Michael's dad had fallen in when they hit and did not resurface. Jimmy was awarded the Mayor's Medal of Honor. He was interviewed by local television. For a number of years, he was asked to speak at the Rotary Club on the anniversary of the crash about how he had only done what anyone would do. What was Robert saying?

"John was not driving when we hit that bolder in the river. He was a far better captain than that. He had just turned the wheel over to Jimmy. You and I were at the back of the boat with the gear, and I looked up in time to see John looking at me as Jimmy was steering. Jimmy looked away at something on the shore. You know Jimmy, always something else on his mind. When he turned to look, his body turned the wheel and we went bow first right into the boulder. I was thrown forward, half out of the boat. The hull was cracked, and we were taking water. You were thrown into the seat in front of you and were knocked out with a bad cut on your head. Jimmy bounced off the wheel and went backwards. John was thrown into the windshield on his left shoulder. We were all dazed. John asked if I thought I could swim. I told him maybe a little, but I was sure my right arm was broken. He said we had to get to the shore because the boat was sinking, and we would be pulled under into the rapids ahead. He grabbed me and we eased over the side. He told Jimmy to stay with you and he would be right back. Somehow, he managed to get us to the rocks on the edge by the Devil's Wash where the water is deep from the river washing it at the turn. He pushed me up on the rocky shore and went back for you and Jimmy. He wanted to bring you first and then Jimmy, but Jimmy got scared. Your dad was pulling you into the water to get you to the shore and Jimmy jumped in, grabbing your dad from behind. Jimmy was flailing around, and your dad went under several times. Somehow, he managed to keep moving toward the shore. As he got near the rocks, he told Jimmy everything would be okay, and with an inhuman shove sort of threw you both onto the rock. But it pushed him under, and he never came back up." Robert stopped and took a napkin from the table to wipe his nose. He was struggling to get the story out.

"Why did we never hear this before?" Michael asked.

"That is the hardest part." Robert cleared his throat and took a sip of water. "It is my fault.

You were unconscious. Jimmy was petrified. I put my head down to rest and guess I passed out from the shock. Some people came running up to help after a while. They saw Jimmy sitting over Michael, holding one of his hands, and they started saying how Jimmy had saved you. Then it grew to saving me too. As Jimmy came around, he just let people say what they wanted. He didn't want to at first, but when he started getting all that attention, he just sort of got into it. He started adding parts that made him look even more like the hero, like the part about John driving the boat. He even wrote that little eBook. And I was the coward. I decided to start drinking because I lost my best friend, and I never told anyone that he was a hero. Not until today."

Michael didn't know what to say. It was like Manny had always said. Something was not right about the story that was told. And now he knew what. His father was the hero. Michael thought a moment, then asked, "Why now? What made you say something now?"

"Well, a little over a month ago, I was really down. Was ready to check out. Instead, I passed out and had a dream." Michael sat up a little straighter as Robert continued. "There was this guy in the dream. He told me all about my life, only at first, I didn't know he was talking about me. He said I could change my life and stop living a lie, and that the truth would set me free. When I woke up, I didn't want to drink anymore. And I knew I had to set things right. I started to clean up my place and make things right with Manny and everyone. You and your mom are the last on my list, but the hardest of all to face." He put his head down as if he was focusing on his coffee, but Michael saw the tears run down and drip off his nose. Michael was still struggling with Robert's story about the dream and the guy in the dream, and how it resembled his own dream, when his mother spoke.

"Robert, we are glad you told us. It must have been difficult all these years. We don't hold any ill will toward you." Emma was trying to console Robert, speaking in a gentle tone as she reached out and took one of his hands. "Do we Michael?" She looked directly at Michael with a look that always melted his heart.

"No, of course not. It was brave of you to come forward with this after so many years." Michael was trying to be encouraging now to Robert. His mother smiled.

"Thank you both," said Robert, holding one of each of their hands in his own. "It means a great deal to me to finally be able to tell you all of this." Robert wiped his nose with a napkin and even managed a glimpse of a smile. The waitress passed by and filled their coffee cups, and Michael noticed that Robert was finishing up some cherry pie. "So, I guess you have some big things going on at work, Michael?" Robert asked.

"How do you mean?" Michael responded, puzzled by the question. He didn't know Robert to pay much attention.

"I spoke briefly to Jimmy a few weeks back. We don't talk much. But he told me about you taking a vacation. He said something about getting a big promotion and how I would be proud of him running things." Robert was beaming.

"As a matter of fact, I think there are some things at work I need to get to now. Will you be okay, Mom?" Michael was processing all of these details. He did not like what they seemed to imply.

"Yes dear, I am fine now. When Robert told me the story, I was just so emotional I ran out to try to find you to tell you. But I am very good now." Emma was back to her old self more now. "Maybe Robert and I will have some lunch, now that we have had desert." Michael smiled and nodded, then headed for the street.

CHAPTER 12:

TIMING IS EVERYTHING

Michael checked his mirrors and the street before doing a quick U-turn to head to the office. His mom and Robert waived as he went by, and he waived back. Robert actually looked good. He looked like the Robert from when he was a child, only older. For now, he needed to get to the bottom of the changes going on at the office.

Michael dialed up the law office again. "Yes, this is Michael Stoneman again. Oh, he did? Yes, that is why I am calling. I will wait." Apparently, Benny had told the receptionist that if Michael called again to get him immediately.

"Hello Michael! I thought you were on vacation. How can we help you today?"

Benny was always the more social of the Silverman brothers. Always had kind words and a smile for everyone. You could hear that smile on the phone now.

"Benny, yes, I am very much trying to be on vacation. I have some loose ends to wrap up. Did you get my message earlier about the company documents? I wanted to get your take on them, especially the stock redemption portion."

"Yes, Michael, I did get your message, and I have been going through them since you last called. The attorney that drew them up must have been a genius, if I do say so myself!" It was Benny that had drawn these up, similar to the ones that he had drawn up for Michael's father years before. "There are some interesting things there in Section 7. Your stock redemption option ends today. Under the option each party can redeem the option shares of the other for themselves for a formulated rate, with a cap at $50,000. This option has certain time restrictions for each party, and shifts over time. Yadda yadda yadda and so on. If you do not exercise your option by the end of today, Jimmy gets the option for redemption for one week, and then the five-year cycle begins again."

"Yeah, that's the way I read it too," Michael commented, somewhat relieved.

"But that is not the really best part, Michael. I pretty much copied over the documents the way your dad always had me do his. What I read you was paragraph A. Paragraph B is another matter altogether!" Michael could tell by tone in Benny's voice that he was particularly proud of this document. "Your dad called Paragraph B the "keep 'em honest" paragraph. He wanted me to write something that said if the first partner makes an offer to buy out the second partner, the second partner has the first option to buy out the first partner for the offering price. Your dad said it would help keep the peace between partners during rough business times. But I don't think he ever used it. He always paid his partners way more than he should have – my brother included, thank you very much!"

"Yes, my father was a different kind of businessman. I keep learning more about him all the time. So, I hear Jimmy had some of your guys in his office today. What was that about? Please tell me he does not have another hair brained scheme about buying up junk properties or something. He has been after me for years to expand my horizons. I just want to do software."

"To be honest with you Michael, I have been wrapped up in some things for my own crazy family. Did you hear about Manny buying an RV from my Jacob? Who would have thought, right? But I can check into it and get back to you if you like." Michael could tell Benny was a little miffed that some of his guys had been to the office and not kept him fully informed.

"That would be great. I will talk to you then Benny. Call me." Michael hung up the call.

Bzz-Bzz. Michael looked at his phone. His mother had sent him a picture of a full chicken dinner at the Diner. The caption read, "Looks like Robert's appetite has returned. Thank you for being so kind today. That's the boy I raised." Michael smiled. It was good to think that Robert was sober and eating again. He had become so thin and sickly looking from the alcohol. Now his phone rang.

Benny's number was on the screen. "Hello Benny. That was pretty fast. What did you find out?"

"Michael, I swear I am going to knock my guys in the head." The stress in Benny's voice was unnerving. He had never heard Benny this way. "Yes, two of my guys were at your place today. Seems Jimmy had them draw up an agreement. I have a copy in front of me here. The title is "Section Seven Purchase" and it looks like he is planning to exercise his option to buy your stock. My guys worded it a little funny – not as clear as it needs to be.

But that is what it looks like to me. And it is what he said to them. Something about using the bonus money you are going to give him to buy you out. I thought I had drawn up your option purchase agreement a month ago. You change your mind or something?" Benny was puzzled that Michael would consider selling.

Michael slowed the car slightly. "No, not to my knowledge." It was a clumsy response, but the words came automatically from Michael's deep-rooted determination not to panic in times of extreme stress. For Michael, this was one of those times. "But I do have a bonus for him this year. I wanted to give him something extra this year. We both agreed that we would not take any bonuses for the first five years. I thought it was a surprise."

"This agreement is for the maximum buy out limit of $50,000." Benny remarked.

"Yes, and that's the number that will be on the cashier's check. The courier will be delivering it this afternoon." Michael was beginning to put the pieces together.

"That's substantial. Can I come to work for you?" Benny never missed an opportunity for sarcastic humor, and somehow it seemed to fit now. "You are a generous soul, Michael."

"Perhaps. But I thought it was a way of saying thank you for a lifetime of loyalty. I am just trying to figure out how this was supposed to go down. Jimmy must have found out from the bank about the bonus. We had discussed my not coming in today and he said we could take care of the paperwork when we got back. I thought we were talking about the Stock Redemption deal that I had you draw up. And Jimmy thought I was not coming in today, because I really was planning to try to get away early. Hmm." Michael's mind was now going 240, as he thought about what he had learned from his mother and Robert, and now this. So, this is why Jimmy was sitting in his chair, and why he told Lilly they would be working together. "Benny, I am going to need you to do a few things and be available by phone. Can you email me a scanned PDF of that document to my personal email address, and send one to Lilly's private email address as well?"

"Absolutely, Michael." was Benny's reply, somewhat drawn out. Michael could tell he was thinking. "I just noticed he had one of my guys notarize it when he signed it. Interesting."

"Why is that interesting?" Michael inquired.

"Well, because they notarized it today. His ability to exercise the option for redemption does not begin until tomorrow. My guys really blew this one. Somebody might not be here next week." There was a tension building in Benny's voice as he thought about the shoddy work his team had done.

"Really? That is interesting." Michael thought for a moment. Suddenly, a serious smile began to creep across his face, like the

Roman general looking over the spoils on the battlefield below where he had just defeated his nemesis. "Benny, I think you need to give that man a raise! I will explain later. And get those emails off as soon as you can, okay? Thanks." He hung up, throwing his phone into the seat next to him. Everything was beginning to add up, and what it was adding up to was more than a little disturbing. "I guess it might be time for a change," Michael muttered to himself as he steamed toward the office.

"Hey, Mo, what are you doing now?" It was Leonard (Lenny) James, the head security guard. Mo (Guillermo) Mejor, the head of maintenance for the entire complex, was bent over some contraption on his workbench. He was always creating something, inventing something, reaching to learn what he did not know.

"It's just a Flux Capacitor, Lenny" was Mo's sarcastic response, not looking up.

"Mo, I know you're just messing with me again. Come on, man, what is it?" Lenny asked showing a genuine interest. He began to reach for one of the silvery globes on the bench, but Mo intercepted his reach.

"It is a scalar wave generator and receiver experimental kit, from Dr. Meyl, if you must know." Mo was half dismissing Lenny and half proud that he had asked.

"Dude, if you need to scale some fish, just ask. I can hook you up with something that's not quite so crazy." Lenny reached into his pocket and pulled out a serious blade.

"What was I thinking," was Mo's reply, shaking his head in disbelief. "I should have just asked." He was smiling from ear to ear, shrugging his shoulders with his hand up just above them.

"Mo, you know I am just messin' with you, man. I don't know what you are doing, but I know it has nothing to do with fish," Lenny smiled, putting away the blade. "Mo, you are like this freaking genius dude, working as a maintenance man for these people. Why do you do that? You could do anything!"

"Well, Lenny, I appreciate what you say." Mo went back to finishing up the experiment. "But you know how it goes. People like me are not supposed to be smart. Most people think I got here in the middle of the night running across the border. Truth is I was born here. But..." Mo shrugged.

"But what?" was Lenny's quick quip.

"But not all of my family here can say the same thing. If I draw attention to me, I draw attention to them." He shrugged again. "It's just the way it works, mi compadre. What about you? You have a lot more talent than watching over the man's stuff here. Why do you stay?" Mo knew the answer, but he also knew his friend liked to talk about it, as he continued to work on the kit.

"Hey, man, I have a plan. I have my own something-something going on the side. My wife and I are working together, and in a couple years I won't be here no more!" It was like he was giving a sermon from the pulpit.

"I believe you, amigo, I believe you. You're special. You will get it done. And you won't have to work for Stoneman anymore," was Mo's response, now wiping his hands and leaning against the bench.

"Hey, Mr. Michael is cool. He helped me and my wife when we had our kid and the insurance folks slow paid us. It's Jimmy that is such a... challenge. That's it, a challenge to work with every day."

"Lenny, that is the most politically correct way you could have said that!" Mo said, laughing.

"And speaking of Jimmy, he is why I came down here. He said for me to come get you to come meet him outside of the private offices.

Has some changes he wants to make. It's crazy man. He always treats me like crap!" The sound in Lenny's voice was both defensive like one oppressed, and angry at the same time.

"Calmete, my brother, calmete! Jimmy's not worth it. He is always making fun of my name. Says I should change my shirts to say "Bill" because it is an American name. The dude is just way shallow. Don't give him the time of day." Mo had put his hand on his shoulder, trying to encourage Lenny.

"Yeah, I know you're right. Like I said, in a couple years I will be outta here! Let's go see what the man wants." Lenny patted Mo on the back, and they headed to yet another discouraging meeting they knew was coming. "You remind me of my man, Al." Mo gave him a puzzled look as they walked away. "Al. You know. Albert Einstein? He said in the middle of difficulty lies opportunity. With Jimmy, we must be headed to the land of opportunity!"   They both laughed as they made their way to the stairs.

Chapter 13:

Times Change - Everything

Michael dialed Lilly's private cell. He had to speak with her before he actually arrived at the office.

"Hello Mary," came Lilly's voice, wavering from some unknown stress. "I am at work dear. I can only take a minute." Obviously, someone was close by Lilly's desk. "She must be trying to hide the fact that she is talking to me," Michael thought to himself.

"Lilly, this is Michael. I am coming in to straighten everything out. Everything will be okay." Michael was trying to be reassuring.

"Oh, I don't know if that is wise dear. I have so much going on here today." Lilly was telling him that they were already taking actions there.

"I understand you cannot talk now. When I get there, I will text you on this number. Benny is sending you..." Michael did not get a chance to finish before Lilly cut him off.

"Michael!" Lilly's voice was muffled to almost a whisper. "I couldn't talk then. Jimmy was standing outside your door with a security guard and a maintenance guy. He was talking about changing the name on the door and some enhanced security cameras. He really talks down to those guys. How are you going to get in here? I think Jimmy told the security guard to stop you at the front lobby."

"Lilly, I am almost there. I will explain more after I arrive. Benny is sending you a copy of an agreement. I need to you to print it off on your printer by your desk. I also need you to get the agreement Benny did for me out of the file. And there will be a second agreement coming from Benny, but that might be after I arrive. I am coming up through the back entrance." Michael's father had an entrance installed after the fact into the "Executive Bathroom" in Michael's office, which was formerly his father's office. Everyone always joked about the bathroom. It was really a refitted oversized utility closet that was just large enough for the full bath installed in it, plus a small clothes rack and the strange door to the outside that had never been used.

"Okay, Michael. I hope that door opens." Lilly sounded concerned, but thoughtful. "Your dad told me when he did it that it would come in really important one day. Told me he got the idea from a dream or something."

There was a strong gust of wind. Michael looked up just in time to hit the brakes. He had just pulled into the parking garage at work. "Wow! Talk about autopilot! I don't remember..." Suddenly, Michael remembered his dream. All of the pieces were coming into play, a little out of sequence. After all, he had made some different choices. It was like the old man said, time is not set. We choose our lives. And the storm of his life was upon him now.

"Lilly, I am here. I have to make a couple quick calls. I will text you once inside." Michael hung up and quickly called the bank. The courier had not left yet but was about to head their way. He instructed the bank manager about several changes in what he needed. Then he called Benny to have him draw up a quick document to email to Lilly. They discussed the details briefly, and Benny knew exactly what to do. Michael grabbed his briefcase and manually locked his Beamer as he got out to keep it from beeping. Walking up to the building he went to the back, taking the back stairs that led, among other places, to the back door of his office. He had the key from his father's possessions on his key ring. He inserted the key. With a deep breath he gave it a turn. It worked! He went in quietly, locking the door behind him.

Sitting at his desk, he noticed a folder in the middle which he had not left there. He shot a quick text to Lilly, "I'm in my office, but don't look this way. I will get back with you in a minute." Michael opened the folder, and there was the original of the agreement that Benny said Jimmy had his guys draw up. Michael poured over the one page "poorly written" document, taking in every word. And there was Jimmy's signature, and today's date. And there was the notary signature from Benny's guy. Michael was smiling that same Roman general's grin, nodding his head. Bzz. Bzz. Michael looked at the text. It was the courier saying he had just arrived and was awaiting instructions as requested. Michael texted him back and told him to come in to deliver the package to his secretary Lilly in five minutes.

"Lilly, the courier is here. He will be coming up to your desk with the package in about five minutes. Where is Jimmy now?" Michael texted Lilly.

"He is interviewing some young man I never saw before behind closed doors in his office." came Lilly's reply.

"Let me guess. A Mr. William Walker?" was Michael's response.

"Yes. How did you know?" was the quick reply from Lilly.

"Long story. I will tell you later. In just a minute I am going to walk out of my office and into Jimmy's office. When the courier arrives, sign for the documents. Then get Lenny up here from Security and print out the second document from Benny. That came in, right?" Michael liked texting, but this was a bit much. Had to make do.

"Yes, it came in. I have already printed it. What is happening?" Even Lilly's texts were beginning to show her stress.

"Everything will be fine. Give me about five minutes after the courier arrives, and come to

Jimmy's office with the documents from the courier, the last document from Benny's office, and your Notary stamp. Have Lenny wait outside the office to the side of the door where he won't be seen when you come in and leave the door open. Can you do that?" Michael realized that he had just put many unknowns into Lilly's head, but she was a trooper.

"Of course I can, Mr. Stoneman. Have I ever let you down?" Lilly was back and she was calm.

There was one last thing he had to do. Looking in the company directory, he dialed the IT Manager's cell phone. "Bobby, this is Michael. Yes, thank you, I will head out soon. I have a priority for you. In exactly five minutes I need you to shut down all of Jimmy's access – computer, Internet, security pass – all of it. I will explain later. No, this is not a drill. Yes. Yes. Okay, thank you."

Michael got up from his desk, placing only the fingertips of both hands on the surface as he leaned forward thoughtfully for a moment. He took a deep breath and sighed. Standing up fully, he picked up the folder with Jimmy's agreement in it and walked toward his door that led to the bull pen of cubicles and other offices. Pausing, he grabbed the knob and said in his "talk to me" voice, "It's show time folks." He opened the door and stepped into the great room layout.

Lilly was smiling and sitting upright. She was busy getting the folders ready. He winked at her and she winked back. As he strode across the great room, he noticed the puzzled looks of those that had seen him emerge from his office without ever entering it. Michael smiled and nodded at a couple of them. "Good morning. You can call me Houdini." Michael was in his best rare form of being the ship's commander, and everyone chuckled lightly, obviously relieved that he was there. At Jimmy's door he tapped on the glass with the closed blinds.

"I'm busy," came a somewhat disgruntled response from Jimmy, inside.

Michael opened the door and went in. "Too busy for me?" Michael asked as he stepped inside. Jimmy sat behind a huge desk his chair tipped back. The young man being interviewed was seated just in front of Jimmy's desk, in a chair that was intentionally built a little lower to the ground than Jimmy's. He was always playing every angle, but today he was caught off guard.

"Michael?" came the stunned reply from Jimmy, holding a Superbowl football he got as a souvenir in his hands. He liked to flash his affluence in many ways when interviewing a new person, and that football was just another in his bag of tricks. "Hey, man, aren't you supposed to be on vacation? Good to see you!"

Michael smiled a polite smile and looked at the young man in the chair. He looked a little nervous and worn out from the grueling process of a Jimmy interview. Michael stuck out his free hand. "Good afternoon. William Walker, right?" A puzzled look and a nod from Walker indicated that he was surprised to see Michael there. "William, be a good fellow and wait for us out in the lobby, won't you please? Lilly will get you coffee or whatever you would like. Thank you."

William had stood up when Michael extended his hand. He left to sit in the lobby, still puzzled by what had just occurred. Michael pulled William's chair over from in front of, to more to one side of, Jimmy's desk. Jimmy's office was very different from Michael's. While Michael enjoyed the older, almost antique looking décor left by his father, Jimmy was just the opposite. His office was very contemporary, from the computerized glass topped desk to the blue tooth ear pieced phone. Michael thought now about how he had appeased Jimmy's whims all these years, even when others questioned it. Of course, he thought he was doing it for a loyal friend and co-worker.

"Do you know Walker from somewhere?" Jimmy inquired. Michael could tell from the look on his face that he was definitely shaken from the surprise visit, and from Michael knowing who Walker was.

"No, I just know someone that knows him." Michael replied without missing a beat. "So, Jimmy, how is your day going? Anything new or important happening that I should know about before I leave on my vacation?" Michael was going to give Jimmy one last out.

"No, just pretty much business as usual. Just another boring Friday afternoon," was Jimmy's reply. "I really am surprised to see you here. Everything okay with that trip I set you up with, buddy?" Jimmy always liked to remind everyone when he did something for them, especially Michael.

"I see. Everything is fine with the trip as far as I know. If you don't have anything to discuss, I have a point or two I would like to go over with you." Michael's face was like stone, his voice unwavering. "I want to talk about the future of the company."

"Okay." Jimmy sat forward and placed the football on the corner of the desk. "Is this about the Silverman deal? Did you get it? How many changes is the old man asking for this time?"

"No, this is not about the Silverman deal. Yes, we got the contract. He did not ask for any changes." Michael responded methodically to each of the questions Jimmy had asked.

"No changes from the old man? Wow! Was he off his meds or something?" Jimmy was trying to be his usual smug self.

"Actually, he said it was about more than just the agreement. He felt that we had always done good work for him and thought it frivolous to argue. Something about loyalty." The intensity if Michael's voice was matched only by his countenance and the piercing in his eyes. It made Jimmy look away briefly. "Loyalty is a good thing, don't you think?"

"Of course it is Michael. If this is not about Silverman, then what is it about?" Jimmy was fidgeting from the conversation.

Just then Lilly walked into the room through the open door. She handed several folders to Michael, but kept her own portfolio in her hands. "You can go," Jimmy dismissively waived Lilly toward the door. She did not move.

"Jimmy, Lilly works for me. I asked her here, and I will let her know when she can return to her other duties." Michael was winding up, and it could be heard now clearly in his voice. "To answer your question, this is about loyalty, or the lack of it." Michael produced the document that Jimmy had Benny's people create and that he had signed, and placed it on Jimmy's desk. "I think this would qualify as something important before I go on vacation, don't you?" Jimmy's face turned red. Michael took out his cell phone, pressed one of the speed dials, and then pressed speaker. The phone at the other end was ringing.

"Benjamin Silverman. How can I help you?" It was Benny's usual greeting of focused customer service.

"Benjamin, this is Michael. I am here with Jimmy and Lilly. I have just shown Jimmy the document he had your people create and he signed today. I also have the one he left on my desk. Can you please explain to us what you shared with me about this document and what it means, given that it was tendered today?"

"Certainly Michael. According to my people this document was crafted primarily by Jimmy. He wanted to exercise his right of redemption on the stock, making him the majority stock holder. My people offered some modifications, which Jimmy rejected. The result is these are Jimmy's words which have been recorded, which he signed, and which my people notarized. Does that sound about right, Jimmy?" Benny was being non-confrontational, but this question was intentional.

"Yes, you are correct Benjamin." Jimmy was now on point, or so he thought. "Michael, your work has been, well, sub-par lately. I cannot let the good people of this company sink with you. I have been saving you and carrying you since we were kids. It is not fair to everyone else here. Under Section 7 of our founding documents, I had the Silverman people draw this up. Sorry Michael, but you are out. We will send your things along. Now, go take your vacation!" Jimmy sat back in his chair as if he had just won a great victory, with his smug little smile.

"I don't think so," was Michael's slow and pointed reply. "Benny, please explain the ramifications of this document, *today*."

"Certainly." Benny cleared his throat at the other end softly. "This agreement does contain an offer to purchase the stock, to purchase the company if you will. It is offered by Jimmy and to Michael. However, it contains no specific wording related to the stock redemption clause of Section 7. Michael's option for the stock redemption does not end until midnight tonight, and Jimmy's does not begin until 12:01 AM tomorrow. Therefore, this is an offer to purchase and not a stock redemption offer. It does contain a price of $50,000 as the offering price. Michael, under Section 7 you can now either accept this offer, or immediately counter and buy out Jimmy for this same amount of $50,000." One could hear the smile on Benny's face at the other end of the phone.

"What are you talking about?! I was exercising my right to the option. Michael is not even supposed to be here. What difference does the date make? Michael, you really need to remove yourself from this office and this building. I don't want to have to call security." Jimmy was picking up the phone and noticed there was no dial tone. With a puzzled look he took out his cell phone, but it would not work either.

"Phone problems Jimmy?" Michael said, smiling. "Not to worry, you do not have to call security. Lenny, could you come in here please?" A very large security guard, ducking slightly as he came through the door so as not to hit his head, stepped in just through the doorway. It was Lenny, the security guard that had been belittled earlier by Jimmy, and he was trying to hold back a smile. "Benny, I am taking out the document I had you prepare. Can you please explain it to Jimmy?"

"Yes. Jimmy, this is the binding counter offer as described in Section 7. Michael is now buying all of your equity in the company for the price offered by you of $50,000. That assumes he has a cashier's check for you in that amount. And of course, he has to sign it and have it notarized." Benny was doing what he does best, clearly explaining contract law.

"I am signing now," was Michael's comment so that Benny could hear. "Lilly, please notarize this signature and the fact that with this document I am presenting this $50,000 cashier's check, made out to Jimmy." Michael produced the check from the courier package that Lilly had given him. She took it, looked at it and the agreement carefully, and then signed and notarized the document. Michael handed the check and the agreement to Jimmy. "One last thing before you go. I spoke with your father just a while ago. I know that all your bravado about saving his life and mine were just a lie. I know that you were steering the boat, not my father. And I know my father was the real hero. Pretenders are really just cowards!"

"I will sue!" shouted Jimmy, jumping up from his chair.

"I hope so. It is about time it became a matter of public record who and what you really are. And I am pretty sure Benny would handle the case personally." There was steel in Michael's voice as he stood to look into Jimmy's eyes.

"Absolutely!" came a comment from Benny, still on speakerphone.

"What about my bonus? And I will need some time to clean out my things." Jimmy began to shuffle through the desk.

"Stop! As for your bonus, here, cash this in or change the names." Michael retrieved the cruise package tickets and contract from inside his suit coat and threw them in front of Jimmy. "I don't need you to plan my time with my family. And as for your things, I will have your successor pack them up and we will get them to you. Leave your cell and your security pass there on the desk, and your keys." Jimmy, still somewhat defiant, dropped the cell onto the desk, then the pass, then the keys. They bounced as they hit, but stayed on the desktop.

"Lenny, could you help this fine young man find the front door?" said Michael waiving to Lenny to escort Jimmy out. Jimmy came around the desk as if he was going to do something foolish walking toward Michael.

Lenny stepped between them. "It would be my pleasure, Mr. Stoneman." Lenny was smiling, but everyone could see the muscles in his arms bulge slightly as he prepared himself for any advances from Jimmy. Jimmy just glared at each of them, one at a time, and then marched out the door with Lenny right behind him.

"Thank you, Benny. I will be in touch." Michael hung up the call and placed his phone in his pocket. "Lilly, I need you to do something for me so I can get on to my vacation. Would you please go through this office and get everything out of here that is not company property? Have it shipped to Jimmy's home?"

"Yes sir, Mr. Stoneman. Why did you give him your vacation? Marie will be crushed to think that you have to stay to find someone to run things while you are gone. I am so sorry." Lilly went behind the desk to begin to empty the drawers. "I don't know where you will find someone that wants THIS décor."

"You are right about the way he decorated this office. I think you should go ahead and get this stuff out of here as well. And make it the way you would want it." Michael had a wry little smile on his face as he picked up his documents folders and other items from next to where he was sitting.

"Okay, I can do that. But what if the new person doesn't like it? That would be a waste of even more money." Lilly was shaking her head.

"Oh, the new person will be well satisfied with how you decorate it." Michael retrieved one more document from the courier package. "Lilly, you are the new occupant. I am promoting you to Executive Vice President, if you will take the job. And it comes with a bonus that I seem to have laying around. Seems the last guy did not earn it." Michael handed Lilly a cashier's check with a memo that said, "Exec. VP Bonus" and it was made out to her for $50,000! The shock and surprise on Lilly's face turned to joy as her eyes became misty, and she nodded in acceptance. "You have pretty much run this place for a while. You will do fine."

Lilly came around the desk and gave Michael a brief hug. "I don't know how to thank you. You and your family have been so good to me all these years."

"And you have been good to us. The truth is Lilly there were times when I thought of quitting early on. Many times it was you and your loyalty to us that gave me the strength to keep going." A breeze blew some of the papers off the desk. Lilly was surprised and walked over to the vent to see if there was something wrong with the HVAC system. Michael smiled. "Don't worry Lilly, it's been like this all day," said Michael, chuckling as he picked up the papers and organized them again.

Getting his things together again, he began toward the doorway. Stopping to turn back to Lilly to give her one last thumbs up, he said, "And you were wrong about vacation, I am still going." Lilly could hear the sound of applause as Michael walked through the bull pen and exited the office.

CHAPTER 14:

THE SALE OF A LIFETIME

There was a pleasant breeze in the air as Michael walked to his car in the parking garage. It was not really a walk, but more like a combination of a march and a victory dance, and he felt light on his feet. "That just feels good. You done good, Michael. You done good," came the self-speak, almost melodiously. He fobbed his way into his car again throwing his burden into the seat next to him. "Okay, Michael, what now? How do you recover from giving away the cruise and still make Marie happy?" As he sat there, he reflected on the day. It had been a busy one but getting Jimmy out and Lilly promoted seemed so right, he wondered what had taken him so long to do it. And the contract with Manny with all that he had said. Michael smiled. He knew exactly what to do next. He pulled out and sped away in the direction of Hwy 55.

There was the gregarious sign, easily seen from the highway. "The Silvermans never do anything small," Michael said to himself as he moved to the exit. The electronic billboard read, "Silverman RV – where your travel journey begins in style." "Jake, you need a real advertising company," Michael thought to himself, shaking his head at the very corny message on the expensive outside display. He rounded the corner as he exited the ramp and pulled into the RV lot.

Getting out of his car and locking it, Michael noticed some RVs toward the front far corner that looked familiar. But why familiar? Then he remembered, they looked similar to the one on the flyer in his dream and to the ones in the brochures that Manny had shown him earlier. Walking down to them, he could tell one was more modern and one was older, but there were similarities to the look and the paint schemes of each. As he drew closer, he noticed signs in the windshield. One read "VINTAGE" and the other "NEW." He noticed the door on the vintage unit was open, so he walked toward it and stepped inside. He was impressed at the condition of what was clearly an older model. There were no signs of wear anywhere, and it even smelled new. It was as if it were on a lot brand new twenty years ago. As his gaze moved toward the living area, he noticed what he assumed was a salesman with his back to him, changing a bulb in an overhead fixture. He was dressed in khaki pants and golf shirt that Michael was sure had the Silverman logo on the front. "I will be right with you sir," the salesman assured him. "just changing out this bulb." As he finished up, the salesman brushed his hands off symbolically, and turned toward Michael. When Michael saw his face, he was shocked.

"Hello Michael! It is good to see you again." The salesman extended his had to shake Michael's. Michael's mouth must have dropped open slightly at his surprise. It was the old man from his dream! "Yeah, yeah. I get that a lot," the old man chuckled as he shook Michael's hand. "So, let me show you around your palace on wheels, your home away from home, the crème de la crème of traveling royalty. Here we have the luxury seating for the driver and his lovely wife as the passenger. Note the fancy button work on the faux leather covers. Overhead we have a spacious bed suitable for both children and adults."

"Excuse me," said Michael as he struggled to regain his grasp on the reality of what was happening. "Excuse me. Aren't you...?"

The old man paused, breaking character for a moment. "Please, Michael, I am trying to sell an RV over here." He smiled as Michael nodded. "You can call me Big Mike." He continued, "Here in the living space we have a luxurious queen-sized hide-a-way sofa bed, a recliner fit for your majesty, and a dining area. This dinette seats six Hobbits or four normal sized people. It also converts into a bed for one or for two people that are very close friends. Moving on to the kitchen area we have all the amenities of home – stove, microwave, refrigerator, freezer, oven, sink with sprayer – the works!" He continued moving towards the back of the RV. "Here we have the full bath with shower. Across the way a stackable washer and dryer suitable for washing all of your daughter's doll's clothing. Back through this door is the master bedroom with two slide outs like up front, a queen-sized bed, and large screen projection television and stereo system." The old man motioned for Michael to return to the front. "So how did I do? Did I make you want to buy one?"

"You were fine. But what are you doing here?" Michael was still bewildcred by the old man being real. The two of them sat in the dinette across from each other.

"Why, I am selling RVs. Just started today. You are my first prospect. I think if you buy, I am going to get a bonus from the boss!" He was smiling and his eyes were twinkling.

"You know what I mean. You were in my dream. All those things in the dream you said happened to you. They happened to me today, or most of them did. Certain things changed, but it was basically the same." There was suddenly that familiar sound of a siren, as it gets closer. Startled, Michael looked around, sitting up a little straighter, then back at the old man with an inquisitive look.

The old man chuckled. "No, Michael, that is really a police siren. You are not asleep." Michael sighed a sigh of relief and relaxed. "I am proud of you Michael. After we met this morning, I was concerned about you being sharp enough to get this far." Michael pulled back, a little put off by the remarks. The old man chuckled again. "Got ya! I'm just kidding Michael. You really do need a vacation to lighten up a bit. I knew you would get here, eventually. That is why I visited you this morning. You have a great capacity for caring, for being creative, for loyalty." There was a gust of wind that rocked the RV slightly.

"Ah yes, the winds of loyalty blow. Anyway, Michael, I knew you would get here because I knew you would figure out what was really important in life. What was really important to you in your life. And you had a busy day. You made Manny's and Benny's days with your accolades to them. You saved your mother's life. You helped heal a repentant old man's heart by listening to Robert's story with forgiveness. You righted a long-term injustice by just using the truth, which will eventually help Jimmy come around as well. And you made Lilly feel more like a contributor to life than you can imagine. All in all, a pretty good day, I would say."

"Yes, but that can't be the end of it, right? I mean, those are all for other people. What about me and my family? I need to help them, I need to help us. I don't know how to do that." Michael was finally realizing just how much of life was passing by.

"Oh, I think you do Michael. If you didn't you wouldn't be here." The old man's voice had that velvety quality like it did in Michael's dream. "And it is about time I get to moving on." The old man stood and moved toward the open door of the RV.

"Big Mike! Wait!" Michael got up and followed him out the door. The door closed behind them as they stopped just outside. "Are you saying the answer is an RV?"

"You are not a brain surgeon, are you kid?" The old man chuckled. "Sorry, I just love that line too much. No, it is not about an RV. It is not about anything you can buy with money. The RV is just a vehicle to get you to what is important; no pun intended. The RV can provide you with opportunity to spend time with those you love, even if it is just parked in your back yard. Remember I told you that others can tell what is important to us by where we spend our time and resources. This RV is a time machine. It can create those beautiful times worth turning into memories that last forever. Like all the items in the treasure chest on my wall. When you made choices different from normal, things changed. Time is not set, not yet."

"Okay. I think I understand. It would be great to have one of those treasure chests like you have. Any chance you can help me get my hands on one of those?" Michael was making light of the situation but was serious deep down.

Big Mike just smiled. "Yes, Michael, I can help you with that. I thought you would never ask. You see, you already have one. It's right here." Big Mike reached out with his right hand and touched Michael's chest just over his heart. Michael jumped slightly as both a warmth like hot chocolate on a snowy day and something like electricity shot through his body from his heart where Big Mike's hand was resting. Big Mike reached out with his left hand and grabbed Michael's right shoulder to steady him. "The things you treasure Michael are always right here, in your heart. And you will always be loyal to the things you treasure most." As Big Mike let go of Michael there was another gust of wind. Michael's mouth was open slightly as he drew in what felt like his first real deep breath in a long time. It felt good.

"Whoa! That was different!" Michael placed his right hand over his heart. "It was like, warm and electric, or something. And I know what I need to do now. Marie, Mel, Johnny, and my Mom – they don't care what we do. They all just want us to be together, to feel that warm electric feeling of building great memories that are timeless." Michael was moving his hands and looking down, then at the horizon as he spoke, like he was doing a business presentation. "So, Big Mike, who are you, really? And how do you do this cool, crazy, great stuff? I mean, you and I, we should go on the road and tell everybody. You could bring that treasure chest and those pieces of paper and wow, everyone would want that, right?"

Big Mike smiled, and reached inside his back pocket and pulled out the formerly rubber banded 3x5 cards, but without the rubber band. "Michael, I am just a simple guy. Not sure about the road show, but I will be around, doing what I do. I just, you know, am who I am, trying to help people one person at a time. It's kind of fun, isn't it?" There was that velvety quality to Big Mike's voice as he spoke. "Always remember, Michael, we will be loyal to what we treasure, and we can choose that. Like a mighty wind in the top of the trees, or that still small breeze just powerful enough to move one feather, loyalty lies waiting for us in our decisions." Big Mike shook Michael's hand, and was reaching to hand him the 3x5 cards with the other. They were both smiling, and for a moment Michael felt as if time really had stopped. But then a huge gust of wind came up just as Michael tried to reach for the cards. He fumbled the hand off a bit, and the cards flew out of Big Mike's hand. Fortunately, they all landed on the steps just inside the door of the RV. But how did the door get open?

"Oh! Man, I am so sorry. Let me get those for you." Michael let go of Big Mike's grip to move into the doorway of the RV, picking up Big Mike's cards. He tried to stack them neatly, then standing turned to hand them back to Big Mike. But he was nowhere to be seen. "Big Mike? Big Mike?" there was no answer, just another gust of wind that threatened to blow the cards from Michael's hands again. He quickly grabbed them, pulling them close to his chest. As he straightened them again, he pulled them away from his body and looked at the top one. He smiled as he read, "Like a mighty wind in the top of the trees, or that still small breeze just powerful enough to move one feather, loyalty lies waiting for us in our decisions." "Yeah, the old man definitely has it going on!" Michael said to himself.

"Hello!" A voice called to Michael from behind. He turned, expecting to see Big Mike. It was a salesman from the lot, but not Big Mike. "My name is Jeff. Would you like to see one of our RVs?"

"Hey thanks Jeff, but Big Mike was already helping me. He and I were just looking at this vintage model." Michael gestured to the RV doorway from which he had just retrieved the cards. Jeff looked puzzled. Michael saw the look on the salesman's face, and followed his gaze to the RV. The door was closed. And it was no longer a vintage unit but a brand-new model, just like the one next to it. "Uh huh. Let me guess," said Michael, staring at the new RV with the salesman. "You don't have a Big Mike that works here either, right?"

"No sir, but we have a Big Jake. He's the owner. Is that who you meant? I can see if he is available." Jeff was trying to be helpful, although puzzled still by the "vintage" comment.

"Yeah, sure. You know what, let's go see Jacob. I think I know exactly what I want." The two of them continued to chat as they walked toward the building showroom. Michael was asking questions of Jeff about his family, and in an out of character way for him, showed true interest in Jeff's answers. And the wind was blowing in gentles pulses, making the banners at the front of the building dance as if there was a hidden tune in the breeze.

CHAPTER 15:

VACATION AT LAST

"Hello? Marie?" Michael called out to Marie as he came through the door, noticing the luggage in the foyer with her hat and sunglasses on top. "You ready to go?"

"Michael!" came the almost shouted response from upstairs, followed by the sound of scurrying footsteps overhead heading for the stairs. "Where have you been? You said you would help me. Now we just barely have time to make it to the airport without missing our flight!" Marie was now almost running down the steps to get to the front door where Michael stood with a silly grin on his face.

"Yes, dear." It was Michael's automatic response.

"Don't 'Yes dear' me Michael Stoneman! I don't want to miss our first real vacation in more than five years. Let's get moving." Marie was half pleading, half barking out orders.

"You are right my love, sorry. But I have some surprises for you." Michael's eyes were lit up like the first time they had gone on a date. Marie stopped cold in her tracks. Michael never stopped the "Yes dear" routine before without her getting angry, let alone apologize for it. Michael stepped to his right to reveal the doorway. At the same moment came two smaller voices shouting happily.

"Hi mommy! Hi mommy!" It was Mel and Johnny, and they were beaming with delight. "Daddy has some surprises!"

"I love surprises!" was Mel's follow up squeal.

"Michael?! Why are the children here instead of at your brother's? There is no way we can drop them off in time before the flight. Is someone with you to watch over them? Did I forget to pack something?" Marie was showing her surprise in her loss of control of the moment, which was rare for her. She rarely used the word, "children" when speaking of Mel and Johnny. She was trying to peer out the door, but the kids had run to her and wrapped their arms around her in a group hug fashion.

"There has been a needful change of plans." Michael was trying to keep a flat tone of voice, and his countenance was solemn as well. But Marie could see his eyes were sparkling.

"What? Is someone sick? Has something happened? Is mom okay?" Marie had reached out with one hand to take hold of Michael's arm to comfort him for what she was sure was about to be very bad news.

"Mom is okay. Yes, something has happened. That is an understatement if there ever was one. Yes, I am sick." Michael began to smirk. "I am sick of always working and never spending time with my family. Going to a great college and learning programming, getting good grades, everybody said it was important. They were wrong. All that got me was more debt! ... And I thought owning my own shop would be the answer. But instead of me owning the business, it felt like the business owned me, like if I don't make everything happen every day, it all falls apart. I had to create the whole thing new every day. I had to be the magic. I'm sick of it. I'm sick of being a performer. I need to be a leader... OF LEADERS. I've had enough of letting my work dictate our lifestyle. ***And as of right now, I'm going to change it! I'm going to find a better way!"***

Marie titled her head slightly, trying to get past her own disbelief of what she was hearing.

BHONK-BHONK!!! It was the sound of what resembled a semi air horn. Just then the RV that Michael had been looking at earlier pulled up, parking in front of the house. On the side near the front was stenciled "the USS Loyalty" over the picture of what appeared to be a pirate's chest. The curb side door opened and out jumped Jeff from Silverman RV. Just then a CTS pulled up behind the RV and parked. Jacob Silverman, the owner of the lot, got out and met up with Jeff as they approached the front porch.

"Michael. Marie. Congratulations on your new dream home away from home, the USS Loyalty. I hope we got that name and image the way you wanted it, Michael." Jeff handed the keys to Michael, who was nodding in affirmation. Jacob shook each of their hands as he continued. "We took a little extra time to test every option on your unit since you said you were going to use it right away. And I had one of my people stock it with your list, Michael." Jacob was very smooth, and customer focused, like his brothers. "Jeff and I need to get running back to the shop. This is the second one of these this week! Business appears to be booming." With a few more quick words of appreciation, Jacob and Jeff gave their regards, got into the CTS and headed back to the lot.

"Michael?" was all Marie could manage to get out, frozen in her stance near the doorway.

"Is that ours, daddy? Is that ours?" Mel and Johnny were again both talking at once. "Can we go look inside?" asked Johnny.

"Yes, the door is open. Go ahead. And get your stuff out of the car to take with, will you please?" Michael pointed to the Beamer. "And no playing with anything in the driver's seat, okay?" Michael had to raise his voice a little because the kids were squealing with delight and almost halfway to the car by the time he finished his sentence. Michael stepped close and put his arms around Marie, who was starting to recover from the shock of the moment. "Who needs the Caribbean anyway? We are going to travel the good old US of A in our own luxury liner and see what the rest of this great country looks like!"

Marie's eyes welled up with tears. She hugged Michael close. "Oh honey! I can't believe it! I feel like I am in a dream." Marie loosened her hug slightly to lean back and ask Michael a question. "But what about mom? She will be so shattered by not getting to spend this week with the kids."

"My dear, you are quite right. But I already thought of that. That is why we are heading over there right now to pick her up to go with us." Michael let go of Marie and stepped toward the luggage. "Now we just need to put these things in the RV."

"Michael, you want your mom to go with us?" Marie asked. Michael nodded as he continued to grab the bags. "But Michael, she has a new puppy. With no advance notice, she won't be able to get the puppy boarded for the trip tonight."

"Yes, my love, you are quite right again. I guess that puppy will just have to join the crew!" Michael was chuckling slightly because he knew how different this must seem to Marie.

Marie took a step back, placing her arms akimbo. With head bobbing side to side, hands on hips, she started in, playfully. "Okay, Michael, that is like the third time you have called me 'My love', which you have not done since we were first dating in college. Now you're telling me you got rid of our vacation in the Caribbean, bought an RV, are going to head across country with the kids for days, having your mother join us, AND going to take her puppy, too?" Michael nodded with an ear-to-ear grin as he had managed to just about juggle picking up all the luggage. "Right. So, who are you and what have you done with my husband?" she said with head wagging and a big grin on her face.

"Very funny, very funny, smartie! How about putting some of that energy into helping with these bags?" Michael was truly enjoying reconnecting with Marie in a way they had not in years, and there was a gentle breeze blowing through the neighborhood. Marie laughed and hugged Michael playfully, causing him to drop a bag or two. She grabbed them and he poked her in the side, laughing as she dropped one of the bags. Finally, they had everything in their arms and Michael headed for the RV where the kids had left their bags outside the door. Marie set the alarm, took one last look around, and closed the door. Picking the two small bags and her purse up from the front porch floor, she headed out to the RV and helped Michael pack the bags into the storage compartments. They embarked on the "Loyalty" and launched away from the curb.

It was a good sixty-minute drive or so to Michael's mom's place. He took that time to recount to Marie the elevator version of all that had transpired from the dream to its manifestation throughout the day. Marie was laughing and enjoying the different parts of the story, and even applauded as Michael told her of interacting with Jimmy and promoting Lilly. They were laughing and teasing, and

Marie even slipped out of her seat to reach over and kiss Michael several times on the journey. The kids were watching videos on the large screen TV and playing some video games. As they drew close to his mother's house, Michael announced his plan.

"Guys, guys..." Michael was getting the attention of Mel and Johnny. "We are going to surprise Gramma, okay? We will park down the street a ways and walk up to the door to talk to her, okay?"

"Yes daddy! I know Gramma likes surprises just like me!" Mel's feet were involuntarily dancing with delight. Johnny nodded and smiled. About three doors down from his mom's was a large enough space, and Michael swept into the parking spot as if he had been parking RVs his whole life. They all got out and headed for his mom's. They were laughing and teasing each other. Michael picked Mel up and put her on his shoulders, which she loved. Johnny took Marie's hand and was half pulling her forward. They arrived at the front door and rang the bell. In only a few moments, the door opened, and Emma emerged onto the porch.

"Michael? What on earth are you all doing here? You have missed your flight?" Emma's concern was clearly written in the beautiful barely visible wrinkles in her face.

"Daddy got us an RV Gramma! It's a surprise!" were the very next words, and they were spoken by the Queen of Secrets, Mel. Johnny looked down and just shook his head. Michael took Mel from his shoulders and set her on the ground with a pinch that made her squeal.

"He did whaaattt?" was Emma's stunned reply.

"That's right mom. Look!" Michael stepped back to give her a clearer view as he gestured to the Loyalty. Michael watched as his mom stepped a step forward, grasped her hands over her heart and sighed. He had not seen her smile like that in a long time.

"Michael, it is a thing of beauty for certain. But what happened to your Caribbean cruise? I thought you and Marie would be on your flight by now. Are you dropping the children off for me to watch?" Emma had some anxiety in her voice, afraid that instead of caring for two energetic grandchildren she would be alone for the next two weeks.

"Well, Mom, anyone can cruise the Caribbean. But our family is going to take a land cruise across the great US of A!" Michael could see that Emma's heart sank as he spoke. "We have just one problem. It seems we are a couple o' mates short! Arrgh!" Michael grabbed her in a hug around the shoulders and did his best pirate imitation. "You and that rascally puppy are bein' kidnapped, me matey, to join us on our adventures! Arrgh!"

"Oh, Michael!" was all Emma could get out. Tears began to run down her face. "You don't want to take an old woman and a pup that is not even house broke on a journey. You and your family go ahead on. We will be fine. Just fine. Besides, we're not packed, I have so many things happening here..." Emma was wiping her eyes and cheeks with her hand embroidered hankie.

"Yer right there madam, no old ladies for us! That's why we're a takin' you and your fierce guard dog." Michael pulled his mom close to hug her, then pushed her back slightly so he could look into her eyes. "Mom, I know this has been a dream of yours since I was a kid. We can throw the dog's little kennel inside the RV, no problem. Just throw a few things in a bag and we can go. If there is anything you need that you do not have, we will just pick it up somewhere. That is what we are doing. If you lock the place up and want someone to check in on it, I already told John what was going on. He said he would stop in every day to bring in the mail and check up on things. All you have to do is say yes."

Emma began to have a few tears again, but she was smiling wide. She nodded her head. "Yes. Okay, let me get some things around." She went in to quickly pack a bag, and Marie followed to help. Mel and Johnny had already freed the puppy from its kennel prison and were playing with it on the front lawn. Michael retrieved the kennel from the back porch and loaded it in the RV. Coming back across the lawn, he jumped at the puppy, who responded by bouncing and jumping sideways as Mel and Johnny lunged to catch him, laughing as they hit the ground. Emma and Marie emerged from the front door, each with a suitcase in hand. "I'm ready, I think." Emma was in a casual sundress and straw hat with sunglasses, and a bright red lipstick smile. Michael had not seen her wear lipstick in years.

With eyes becoming misty, Michael jogged to the porch and, taking the bag from her hand, gave his mother a hug, saying "I love you, Mom." "I love you too, son," was her whispered reply. Michael kissed her cheek and stood upright, taking the other bag from Marie. "If you ladies would be so kind as to lock up here, we need to get aboard the USS Loyalty so we can shove off and get on to our magnificent land cruise!"

Emma and Marie laughed, and they briefly went in to set the alarm. Quickly returning to the front porch, Emma locked the doors behind her. They headed for the coach, with Mel and Johnny finally capturing the dog to carry him on board, squirming with a tongue that flapped in the breeze. With everyone on board, Michael closed the door and took his place behind the wheel. "Okay everyone, there is a campground just a couple hours or so from here. We should be able to make that before sundown. We could go there and get our site and get a nice fire going before dark. They have a small water park we can use for free and cool stuff all weekend. After that we can head to wherever we want to go. Sound good to everyone?"

"Yeah!" Mel and Johnny squealed at the same time. The kids were in the dinette, and Marie and Emma had taken a seat on the couch. They were smiling at the amazing transformation today had on Michael. Looking at each other, they shrugged their shoulders and their heads bobbed, and Marie gestured a pinch of her arm as if to say, "Am I dreaming?"

"That sounds great to me, honey. Mom, I think you should have the honor of being the first to ride in the passenger seat. This has been your dream forever. I will get something around for us to eat for dinner and stay with the kids and this cute dog."

Emma's eyes lit up with excitement! "Okay," she said, nodding and getting up to head to the plush seat of honor next to Michael. She got buckled in and they pulled away from the curb. Marie found the supplies that Michael had placed in the fridge. Chicken salad, bread, juices, potato salad and more – the works! She prepared some sandwiches and cold plates while the kids occupied themselves with cards and a dog that thought he was in a velvet painting. They made their way out of the city to the interstate. Once there, Michael felt the urge to share with his mom all that had transpired, but he didn't know where to start. Then Emma said something very odd.

"It's like a dream come true," Emma remarked. "I guess dreams really can change things."

"That is an interesting comment. How do you mean that, Mom?" Michael asked.

Emma just smiled. "When times like this happen, it just reminds me of things from a long time ago." She looked down at her lap for a moment, thinking, and then looked back out the windshield. "It is so beautiful to see everything from this seat. You said we have a couple hours on the road?" Michael nodded. "Well, dear, why don't you tell me about your day, and how you managed to change your mind about... well, so many things all at once?" Emma turned her head to   face Michael as she finished.

Michael's forehead squeezed a questioning look as he cast his gaze at Emma briefly. Smiling, he turned back to concentrate on driving while he talked. "What does she mean?" he thought to himself. "Does she somehow know about the dream?" After today, he guessed anything was possible.

"Well, Mom, it is funny the way you mention a dream. This really all started from a dream I had last night." Michael glanced at Emma, who was looking out the windshield still. He thought she might be shaking her head, thinking he was crazy. Instead, she smiled and nodded. "Okay, so you don't think I am crazy. That's a good start. So, let me begin with the dream and then tell you how the day seemed to... well it seemed to sort of 'fit in' to the dream, or something. I don't know. It sounds crazy when I say it out loud like that."

"No, dear, it's not crazy at all," was Emma's reply. "Go on."

"Okay. Here goes. I had this dream that I was driving in to work, and I came across this bum, only he wasn't a bum." For the next two hours Michael shared his story. Marie brought them their cold plates of food to eat as Michael drove. Emma asked questions and made comments from time to time. They laughed and they almost cried at various parts of the story, especially when they spoke of Michael's father. Just as they were finishing the recounting of the day, Michael pulled off the highway and soon was at the park entrance. He had registered online and was able to drive directly to their site as a result. As they set up, he opened the app for check-in on his phone. The kids were playing with the dog on his leash, and Michael was getting the fire started. It would soon be sundown. The ladies were unpacking chairs to set up around the campfire when the camp ranger pulled up.

"Hello everyone. My name is Bill and I am the ranger on duty." He handed them an information sheet. "If you need anything, my cell is on there. Security's cell is on there as well. You can also call them. I see you are pretty well settled in. If you like, I can put you on the all-night fire list and our security people will throw a log or two on the fire during the night as they drive around. A lot of folks that come here from the city like to be able to see their fire burning all night and have it ready for cooking in the morning when they come out for the weekend. Or at least, many like that the first night. There is no charge. Is that something you're interested in having us do?"

"Bill is it?" Michael extended his hand and the ranger nodded, shaking his hand. "I am Michael, this is my wife Marie and my mother, Emma. These two are my rambunctious kids, Mel and Johnny." Bill tipped his hat to each one. "Bill, we would love to have you do that for us. We have been traveling a while and it has been a long day.

We will likely be turning in soon. But the idea of having a fire ready for cooking in the morning or to just look out and see it is awesome. Thank you!"

"Our pleasure," smiled Bill. He tipped his hat again. "Ladies," and then got back in his Jeep and drove off. By now the fire that Michael had built was going strong, and the sun was setting. The kids came closer to the fire, sitting on the ground with the dog between them. Marie, Michael, and Emma all sat in chairs behind them, looking into the fire.

"Well, my love, I guess this isn't the cruise you were expecting. I hope you enjoy it." Michael's voice was almost apologetic.

"Are you kidding? I love it! This is the most exciting, most romantic trip we have ever taken. And to have Mom and the kids here... and the dog (she chuckled) just make it sooo perfect! Thank you so much, honey. This is precious." Finishing setting Michael straight, she leaned over and kissed him. "I have had a long day. I think I will go in and get cleaned up to turn in. Do you want me to put the kids down first?"

"Oh my, no dear," was Emma's immediate response. "If we were at my house, I would do that for them. They are enjoying the fire. I will bring them in an hour or so. I thought they could sleep in that dinette space with the dog and I could take the hide-a-bed, if that is okay."

"Sure Mom, that sounds great!" Marie stood and then leaned over to kiss Michael again. It was a somewhat lingering kiss, with her hand beside his one cheek. "Will you be joining me soon?" she asked with an inviting smile.

Michael smiled. "Absolutely." With that, Marie disappeared into the RV to clean up from the journey. "I am the luckiest man in the world, Mom. Marie held on all these years while I lost focus on what was important. Never again."

"Yes, you are, Michael. You and your father were always so much alike. Even more so now." Emma was wistfully recounting something from the past, looking into the fire as she spoke.

"In what way do you mean?" Michael asked, inquisitive about the "even more so now" comment.

"When your father and I were first married, he was just starting in insurance. He worked long hours and traveled a lot. Even after you were born, he was relentless in the pursuit of making his agency a success. Then, like you, he had a dream. Everything changed. And he even knew that one day he would give his life for yours..." Emma could not go on for a moment. Michael took her hand.

"What do you mean? Did dad have a dream with an old man in it that he met in real life? What are you saying?" Michael was only beginning to realize that just when he thought he had it figured out; he was discovering another layer of mystery.

Emma smiled and turned to look at Michael. "We have the next two weeks to tell you all of that, but yes is the short answer. When your father told Manny because they were best friends, it really shook Manny up. That eventually led to him and Robert and the others leaving. I never told you because many people said so many bad things about him after the accident..." Emma's eyes gave away her deep emotions. "Anyway, we can talk about that later. I believe you have a lovely wife waiting for you on board. I will look after Mel and Johnny and get them to bed in about an hour or so. You go on now." Emma smiled and motioned Michael toward the Loyalty. Smiling, he got up and kissed Emma on the cheek, and headed for the RV.

Once inside, he went to the refrigerator and retrieved a bottle of champagne he had purchased for the trip. It was just one of his several surprises he had in store for Marie.

He also found the box he had "hidden" that said "Michael's: Keep Out!" which contained strawberries hand dipped in dark and milk chocolate. From the cupboard he found a small glass serving dish for the strawberries and the two glasses he had purchased earlier that day, etched with His and Marie's names. On Marie's glass were also the words, "My love, forever." He placed all of these on a serving tray and laid a dish towel over his left arm. Michael walked up to the door to their room. He knocked lightly. From within he could hear Marie invitingly say, "Come in." He entered the room, closing the door behind him. The day that had started as a dream that changed their hearts forever, continued to unfold into an adventure. It was the adventure that became their love and their life together, heard of and longed for by many, but experienced only by the few that would choose the winds of loyalty. What will we choose?

"In the middle of difficulty lies opportunity."

-*Albert Einstein*